D0436387

J MYS
Wright, Betty Ren.
Out of the dark
New York : Scholastic,
c1995.

09

Discarded by
Santa Maria Library

GAYLORD MG

OUT OF THE DARK

OUT
OF THE
DARK

BETTY REN WRIGHT

SCHOLASTIC
HARDCOVER

Scholastic Inc.
New York

Copyright © 1995 by Betty Ren Wright

All rights reserved.
Published by Scholastic Inc.
SCHOLASTIC HARDCOVER is
a registered trademark of Scholastic Inc.

No part of this publication may be reproduced
in whole or in part, or stored in a retrieval system,
or transmitted in any form or by any means,
electronic, mechanical, photocopying, recording, or otherwise,
without written permission of the publisher.
For information regarding permission, write to Scholastic Inc.,
555 Broadway, New York, NY 10012.

Library of Congress Cataloging-in-Publication Data

Wright, Betty Ren.
Out of the dark / by Betty Ren Wright.
p.   cm.
Summary: When Jessica moves to her grandmother's childhood
home and makes friends with the handicapped girl next door, she
begins to have nightmares about the old schoolhouse
in the woods.
ISBN 0-590-43598-1
[1. Nightmares—Fiction.   2. Grandmothers—Fiction.   3. Physically
handicapped—Fiction.]
I. Title.
PZ7.W933Ou   1995
[Fic]—dc20   93-48025
                                                        CIP
                                                        AC

12 11 10 9 8 7 6 5 4 3 2 1   5 6 7 8 9/9 0/0

Printed in the U.S.A.   37

First Scholastic printing, January 1995

For
Renee Houte

Out
Of the
Dark

CHAPTER ONE

She walked alone through dense woods, thinking of Hansel and Gretel, who had found a witch at the end of a path like this one. Don't be dumb, she told herself, it's really nice here. It's pretty. Bars of sunlight poked through the arching trees, and birds sang. Nothing to be afraid of. Then she looked over her shoulder and discovered that crisscrossing branches had formed a wall behind her. She couldn't turn back.

The path grew darker. She began to cry, which was weird, because even though she was often scared, she never cried. She knew something was waiting for her around the next curve, or the next, and she didn't want to find out what it was.

She reached the edge of a clearing. Meadow grass covered the ground, and daisies were scattered around like bits of sun. On the far side of the clearing was a small building. Its white paint was peeling. An empty bell tower rose over the entrance on one side, and there were flower boxes at the windows.

She thought, It's just a little old schoolhouse! Nothing to be afraid of. But her mouth was dry, and her fists were clenched so tightly that her nails cut into her palms. She sobbed louder, unable to stop. Then, as she stared across the clearing, the shabby door opened, inviting her inside. She was going to have to cross the clearing, climb the wooden steps, and go through that door into the darkness beyond —

"For goodness' sake, Jessie, wake up!"

Jessica Belland swept away spiderwebs of sleep and looked up at her mother.

"I was dreaming," she said. "It was awful!"

"Must have been." Mrs. Belland nodded briskly. "I could hear you all the way downstairs in the kitchen."

"I don't know why I was so scared," Jessie began, but her mother was already out the door. For months now she'd always been in a hurry, with a look that said, better than words, that she didn't want to hear anyone else's problems.

"Get dressed right away, Jess," she called back over her shoulder. "I have to be at work at ten, and I'm going to drive into town for groceries first. I want you to come with me and help find things in the store."

Jessie sat up and filled her eyes with what was real, trying to forget the frightening dream. She was in her grandmother's blue-and-green bedroom, the prettiest room Jessie had ever slept in. Grandma's photographs, enlarged and framed, hung on the walls, and there was a portrait of Grandma Belland herself when she was a girl.

Looking at the portrait is almost like looking into a mirror, Jessie thought. She and Grandma could be twins. They had the same dark, curly hair, the same thinnish nose, the same wide-set brown eyes.

And they were best friends, even though they didn't see each other very often. Grandma Belland *knew* things. She knew how frightened Jessie had been when her mother and dad lost their jobs six months ago. She knew how Jessie worried when her parents looked sad and whispered about money problems. She knew how hard it had been to move across St. Louis to a smaller apartment, leaving school and friends behind. Just when Jessie was sure she couldn't bear it all another minute, she'd find a letter in Grandma's graceful hand-writing waiting for her when she came home from school. *Don't give up, Jessie*, it would say. *Don't you dare give up!* Jessie would read and reread each letter until the next one came.

She wished her grandmother was with her right now, to hear about the scary dream. But if she was here, we wouldn't be, she reminded herself. Grandma was a hundred miles away, settling into

her new job as assistant to the State Superinten-
dent of Schools. The house was theirs only tem-
porarily, a wonderful gift to be enjoyed for the next
two years, maybe longer. Grandma had said they
would be doing her a favor if they would live in it
while she was in Madison.

It was like her grandmother to say that, Jessie
reflected, as she pulled on yesterday's jeans and
top. As if she hadn't practically saved their lives
by making her offer when she did!

"Jessie, will you hurry up — oh, there you are."
Her mother, sitting in the cheerful breakfast nook,
glanced up briefly and then returned to her grocery
list. Jessie's father sat next to the window and
stared out, just as he often did at home.

Only now he has trees and fields and a garden
to look at, Jessie thought happily. Her spirits rose
as she slid onto the bench beside him. The house
was tucked into a hillside with a long slope in front
and flower beds on every side. The windows of
their apartment in St. Louis had looked out at gray
brick walls.

"It's nice!" she said softly. "Are you getting in-
spired, Dad?"

"Sure thing." Mr. Belland grinned. "If I can't do
it here, I'll never do it anywhere."

"It" was the book he was going to start this
summer, all about his experiences in Vietnam long

4

ago and with the veterans' support groups he'd been helping to organize ever since. The book was the main reason they had accepted Grandma Belland's invitation. And it was one of the reasons Jessie's mother was grim-faced as she checked over her grocery list. Jessie's mom didn't believe in the book. She'd wanted them to stay in St. Louis and continue looking for jobs. Instead, they had traveled here to the Wisconsin countryside, where there would be no rent to pay, but where the only available job for Mrs. Belland was a low-paying clerk's position at Andersen's Hardware in Willow, five miles away.

"Well, I hope the scenery helps," Mrs. Belland said tartly. "Because our meals certainly aren't going to be much. We're going to eat a lot of hamburgers on what *I'm* earning."

"Nothing wrong with hamburgers," Mr. Belland said. "Food for the gods." But he looked depressed, and Jessie wished her mother didn't sound so cross. She knew her mom was worried about expenses, but her dad was worried, too. It must be hard to write a book. Just thinking of the thick pack of white paper waiting next to the typewriter on the screened-in side porch was enough to give Jessie goosebumps. She wondered if the thought gave her father goosebumps, too.

Later, as they drove into town in the old blue

5

Chevy, she tried to talk to her mother about the book, but as usual Mrs. Belland changed the subject.

"Your job is to stay out of your father's way while he's writing," she said. "I know it won't be easy, but that's the way it is. You'll miss your friends — "

"Gwen has to baby-sit all summer," Jessie interrupted. "And Emily's going to California to stay with her dad. I *wanted* to move here, Mom, honest."

"What are you going to do today?"

Jessie shrugged. "Look around, I guess." She pointed at a birchwood arch that curved over a narrow road on their left. "Look at that sign. It says 'Willow Township Nature Preserve.' Maybe I'll go exploring there."

"By yourself?" Her mother frowned. "I don't think you should wander very far from the house alone, Jess. You don't know the first thing about country living. Nor do I," she added. "But it looks as if we're about to learn, whether some of us want to or not."

The town of Willow was no more than three blocks long. Most of the houses were tiny, and they looked even smaller because of the giant willow trees that towered over most of them. Mrs. Belland parked the car next to Carlsons' Supermarket on the highway, and they went inside.

To Jessie's surprise the store was bigger than the one where they shopped at home. Lots of people besides the residents of little Willow must do their shopping here, she decided.

"Best time to come, obviously," Mrs. Belland murmured, as they rushed up one aisle and down another. "No one to get in the way." It was only a few minutes before they were at the checkout counter, where the man at the cash register looked at them with curiosity.

"You folks moving into town? Don't suppose you're just passin' through. Visitors don't usually buy this kind of stuff — flour and baking powder and such."

Jessie's mother nodded. "We're staying at the Belland place while Mrs. Belland's in Madison. She's my husband's mother. We *live* in St. Louis, actually."

The storekeeper reached across the counter to shake her hand. "Great lady, your mother-in-law!" he exclaimed. "We're all proud of her. And this is your daughter? She sure looks like her grandma. Think you're going to like living in the country, young lady?"

"I'm afraid Jessica's going to be pretty lonely till school starts," Mrs. Belland said, before Jessie could reply. "I'll be working, and her father — well, he'll be busy, too. I can't imagine what she's going to do with herself till school starts."

7

The storekeeper put the last of their purchases into a paper bag. "You have a neighbor about your age," he told Jessie. "Toni Draves is the name. Don't know if you two would hit it off. . . . Never do know with kids."

"How old is he?" Jessie asked eagerly.

"Not he — she. Short for Antonia, or some such. She's twelve or thirteen, I'd guess. Her dad has the farm right next to the Belland place — his wife's folks worked the place before him. He's widowed now, keeps pretty much to himself. Must be kind of lonely for the girl — she doesn't come into town much." He lifted the last of the paper sacks into the cart so they could push it out to the car. "Wouldn't hurt to try her, I s'pose," he added doubtfully. "Good luck to you."

"Can we stop at the Draves' house on the way home?" Jessie asked, when they were back in the car. "Just for a minute, I mean."

Mrs. Belland shook her head. "I have to unload the groceries and be back in Willow in forty minutes," she said, then relented when she saw Jessie's expression. "I could drop you off at the Draves', I suppose. You'll have to walk home afterward."

"Okay." Jessie didn't much like the idea of introducing herself to strangers without her mother to back her up, but she knew it was no use arguing. "Maybe I'll ask what's her name — Toni — if she wants to go for a hike in that nature preserve."

"Probably old hat to her if she's lived here all her life."

Watching her mother's taut, unhappy profile, Jessie felt a return of the uneasiness that had followed her nightmare. By the time the car stopped in front of an old red barn, she had almost changed her mind about getting out.

"Well, this is it." Mrs. Belland's fingers drummed on the steering wheel. "Draves' farm — there's the name on the mailbox."

"But where's the house?" Jessie wondered. "There's nothing here but a barn and silos and stuff."

"I think you have to go along that little road and past the line of trees." Her mother pointed at the rutted lane that led around the barns and up a gentle hill. "It must be back there. They probably wanted to put some distance between the house and the animals." She looked with distaste at the muddy barnyard where a half-dozen black-and-white cows watched them. "Come on, Jess, make up your mind."

"I'm going." Jessie opened the car door and slid out. "See you tonight, Mom. I hope you like your job."

"Thanks." The car shot away, sending a spray of gravel over the blacktop highway. Jessie watched until it turned into Grandma Belland's driveway. Then she started up the road past the barn.

As her mother had thought, the house was on the other side of a row of towering blue spruces. It was small and neat, its windows closed and curtained. As Jessie hesitated in the front yard, one of the curtains twitched. She climbed the steps to a porch that was only slightly wider than the door, knocked lightly, and waited.

When the response came it was so startling, and so close — right on the other side of the door — that she jumped backward and almost tumbled off the little porch.

"If the school asked you to come here, you can tell them to forget it," the voice snarled. "I'm not going back there, ever!"

CHAPTER TWO

"I don't know anything about your school." Jessie heard the quiver in her own voice, and it made her angry. "My name is Jessica Belland. I live next door. We just moved in." She glared at the closed door. "Don't worry, I'm leaving."

She thumped down the steps and was halfway across the yard when she heard the door open behind her.

"It's okay," said the husky voice. "You can come in. If you want to."

The girl in the doorway was a head taller than Jessie, with light-brown hair that hung straight to her shoulders. Her face was narrow, with big dark eyes and heavy brows. She looked as if she'd like nothing better than to close the door again, but she was curious, too.

"It doesn't matter," Jessie said coolly. "I just thought maybe you'd like to go for a hike. Or something."

"Come on in." The girl turned and went back into the house with a clumsy, rocking step. Jessie stopped at the doorway, hating to leave the bright sunlight for the dim little room in front of her. The girl sat down on a couch. She tucked her legs under her quickly, and there were pillows propped around her to form a cozy nest. At the other end of the couch a large orange cat was curled in a ball.

When Jessie came in, the girl pointed a remote control and switched off the television sound but not the picture. "Sorry I yelled at you," she said. "When I started middle school last year, the teachers kept finding friends for me, and I hated it. I thought maybe they sent you — someone must have. Who was it?"

Jessie perched on the edge of a chair. "A man at the supermarket said there was someone my age living next door to us," she said. "He didn't *send* me."

Toni Draves sniffed. "That's Mr. Hogard. His daughter's in my class. She's a snob."

They stared at each other. "Why did you think someone must have sent me?" Jessie asked cautiously.

Toni remained silent for another moment. Then, she thrust her left leg out straight. "Because of *that*," she grated. "As if I couldn't make my own friends — if I wanted them."

Jessie looked at the misshapen shoe partly hidden by Toni's baggy jeans. The shoe was wide and was laced tightly over a bulging instep. The heel and sole were more than an inch thick.

Oh, no! Jessie thought. And I asked her to go hiking!

Toni was watching her intently. "Go ahead and stare," she said. "It doesn't bother me."

"I didn't mean to stare," Jessie protested. "I just — it's not — "

"It's not important," Toni finished the sentence for her. "Of course," she added venomously, "it would be *very* important if it was *your* foot, wouldn't it?"

Jessie stood up. "I have to go," she said. "My dad'll be looking for me. Sorry I bothered you."

Toni rose, too, her fingertips resting lightly on the arm of the couch for balance. "Where do you want to hike?" she demanded gruffly. "Or have you changed your mind?"

Jessie shrugged. She'd changed her mind, all right, but she didn't know how to say so. "I saw a nature preserve sign when we went to town. . . ."

"Do you have a bike?" Toni smiled with satisfaction at Jessie's look of surprise. It was a smile that said, quite clearly, Of course I can ride a bike, dummy.

13

"I have my grandma's. She said I can use it while we're living here."

"Well, I'll go with you tomorrow then," Toni announced, as if she were granting a great favor. "We'll ride over there and leave our bikes at the entrance — they don't want bikes or dogs on the trail. Come about ten — I'll be busy till then."

"You don't have to — " Jessie began, and then she gave up. "Okay, see you tomorrow."

I should have told her to forget it, Jessie thought unhappily as she made her way down the lane to the highway. Somehow, at the very moment she'd been about to escape, she'd been trapped. Now she'd have to spend more time with this bad-tempered neighbor.

The field between the Draves' barn and the edge of Grandma Belland's property was stitched with neat green rows that Jessie's father had identified as soybean plants. Tiny white butterflies danced among them, and overhead a huge bird dipped and glided. Gradually, as she walked, the tightness in Jessie's shoulders eased and her steps grew lighter. She wasn't going to let Toni Draves spoil this beautiful first day in the country.

When she reached the house, there was no sound from the side porch where her father was working. She opened the back door quietly and tiptoed into the kitchen. The table in the breakfast nook was crowded with canned goods, jars, and cereal boxes. A note was propped on one of the boxes.

Jess, I put away the frozen things — you do the rest. Hope your visit went okay. It's fun to meet new people — good experience for you.

Mom

Fun! Jessie stifled a groan, remembering Toni's resentful expression. Walking on a sunny day was fun. Living in Grandma Belland's house was fun. But meeting Toni Draves had *not* been fun. More often than not, she thought ruefully, when your mother said "it's good experience," you'd better hold onto your hat and get ready for trouble.

CHAPTER THREE

Dinner was on the screened-in porch that evening. Mr. Belland shifted his typewriter to an end table to make room for chicken casserole, green beans, and sliced tomatoes.

"Let's eat out here every night," Jessie suggested. "It's as good as a picnic — without the flies!"

Her mother smiled wanly. "Feel free to set the table wherever you want," she said. "Right now I'm almost too tired to eat. I've been on my feet all day and feeling totally stupid most of the time — ugh! I really don't know what I'm doing in a hardware store. I never could tell a screwdriver from a wrench, and I never wanted to."

"You'll be an expert before you know it," Jessie's father assured her. But he said it as if he really weren't paying attention. His eyes kept turning toward the folder on the table next to the typewriter, as if he'd spent *his* day in another world and hadn't quite made it back. No one mentioned the book, but Jessie saw her mother glancing at the folder, too.

Mostly they ate in silence, with bird song for background music and with one surprise visit from a squirrel who scrambled up the screen and rattled the doorknob.

"That girl next door is really rude," Jessie said finally, when she realized no one was going to ask about *her* day. "I don't think she wants any friends."

Mr. Belland blinked. "What makes you say that?" he asked. "Who wouldn't want Jessica Rose Belland for a friend?"

"You should have heard her," Jessie said. She described her visit. "We're going hiking tomorrow," she finished, "but I'd rather go alone. Or stay home and read. She's the prickliest girl I've ever met."

"Well, you can't spend your whole life hiding in a book," Mrs. Belland said sharply. "Be understanding, Jessie. The poor girl obviously thinks no one likes her because she's different. She's ready for a fight, because she doesn't want to be hurt."

"But that's dumb," Jessie protested. "What's her foot got to do with whether people like her or not?"

Her mother stood up and started gathering their

17

plates. "I seem to remember when you couldn't get dressed for school in the morning without phoning your best friend to find out what she was going to wear. You couldn't bear to be even a little bit different."

"That's not the same thing," Jessie protested.

"Sure, it is. Looking like everyone else was the most important thing to you. Think about it — and while you're thinking, help me fill the dishwasher."

Her mother's words rattled around in Jessie's head all evening, through two sitcoms and a game of Scrabble. Maybe it was true that Toni's anger was just a cover-up for her real feelings. But when Jessie went up to bed she still wished she'd told her neighbor she'd changed her mind about the hike. Better yet, she wished she'd never gone to the Draves' farm in the first place.

When she finally fell asleep, the nightmare was waiting for her, more frightening than ever.

Once again she was walking along a forest trail. The path was darker than before; patches of sky, visible through the treetops, were a dirty gray. Jessie wanted desperately to turn back, but she couldn't. The path kept closing behind her.

She reached the clearing. This time there was no sunshine to brighten the scene before her. The little schoolhouse looked eerie and forbidding. As she stared, the door opened slowly and a young woman stepped out onto the porch. Her knee-length dress made a splash of brilliant blue against the shabby white wall, and there was a wide blue ribbon holding back her blonde hair. She could have been beautiful, but when she saw Jessie her face twisted with rage. With her eyes fixed in an unblinking glare, she crossed the porch and drifted down the steps. Jessie panicked. She tried to push through the wall of branches and underbrush behind her, but there was no escape, no place to run.

She woke to the sound of a chipmunk scolding just outside the window. From downstairs came the comforting clink of dishes. The toaster popped.

Jessie scrambled out of bed and hurried across the hall to the bathroom, stumbling in her haste. Don't think about it! she ordered herself. Forget it! She splashed her face with cold water and raked a comb through her hair. Then, still in her pajamas, she raced downstairs to the kitchen.

Her father looked at her curiously. "Your mom went to work early," he said. "She says she needs some extra time to get used to the stock. Did you sleep all right?"

Jessie slid onto the breakfast-nook bench and

gulped the orange juice he'd poured for her. "Okay."

"You look sort of . . ." he shrugged, "sort of rattled."

"I had a dream about walking in the woods," Jessie said. She knew the words didn't even begin to explain the way she felt.

"Not surprising, I guess."

Jessie looked at him.

"Since that's what you're going to do today," Mr. Belland explained. "You and our neighbor are going to take a walk in the woods. Right?"

"Right." Jessie watched a hummingbird, half the length of her finger, hover over a red petunia. She counted the number of birds fluttering around the birdbath. If you filled your head with other things — pleasant things — you could crowd out what was scaring you.

"Look at that cloud!" she pointed. "It's shaped like a hippo. And the little one behind is sort of like our car."

Her father grinned at her. "You have an excellent imagination," he said. "Eat your cereal."

Later, he went out to the garage with her and helped her lift Grandma Belland's ten-speed from its rack. "Good luck," he called, as she sailed down the drive to the highway. "Maybe your friend will surprise you."

Jessie didn't think it was likely. "Good luck to you, too," she called back. When she turned onto the highway he was still standing there watching her, his hands in his pockets. He looked as if he might be trying to think of other things, too, she decided — something besides his book, maybe.

Toni Draves was waiting at the barnyard fence that edged the road. Her bike was propped against the mailbox.

"What's so funny?" She scowled as Jessie skidded to a stop beside her.

"You've got company." Jessie pointed at the large black-and-white cow peering over Toni's shoulder. "What's her name? I think she wants to make friends."

"She's not a friend," Toni said. "She just works here."

At that, the cow turned and ambled across the barnyard, her hoofs squishing noisily in the mud, her ropy tail swinging. She looked so insulted that both girls laughed.

Maybe this'll be all right after all, Jessie thought, as they skimmed along the highway. Toni led the way. She went very fast; if pedaling was painful for her, she wasn't about to let Jessie know it.

When they reached the birchwood arch that

marked the entrance to the nature preserve, they slid off their bikes and walked them across the little parking lot to the bike stand.

"This whole place belonged to a family called McNaughton," Toni offered as she crouched to lock her bike. "They weren't farmers, they just liked living in the country. The last two members of the family were sisters, and they lived in a big house beyond the woods until they died. Then they left the whole estate to Willow Township for a nature preserve. They even left money for signs and stuff. It's supposed to be kept safe for any animal that wants to live here — no picnics, no ball games, no noise. I guess we're the only visitors today," she added.

"Where do we start?" Jessie wondered.

"There are two or three trails, but most people start right there." Toni pointed across the parking lot. "That one cuts right across the estate."

Jessie looked at the opening in the trees and tried to ignore the shrinking feeling in her stomach. *Of course it reminds you of the dream!* she scolded herself. *Does that mean you're never going to walk in woods again as long as you live?*

Entering the trail was like stepping from one world to another. Wildflowers, pink, lavender, and yellow, edged the path, and the woods on either side were alive with the buzzing of insects and the songs of birds. Jessie took a deep breath and felt her fears begin to fade. She glanced at Toni and saw that her companion's expression had softened.

"Those are wild orchids." Toni nodded toward a patch of delicate pink and purple. "See, that little sign tells you about them. And that's a bee tree up ahead. I saw a raccoon climbing it once. Or else — " she looked at Jessie slyly — "it might have been a small bear, I suppose."

"A bear!" Jessie exclaimed. "What did you do?"

"Kept walking," Toni said. "What else?"

Jessie knew she was being teased, but she didn't care. This was a different Toni from the one she'd met before. She was a good guide, pointing out flowers and ferns with as much pride as if she'd planted them herself.

"Here's a mayapple," she said and lifted a small umbrella of leaves so Jessie could see the single yellowish fruit underneath. "They taste pretty good — sort of like strawberries. But the rest of the plant is poisonous."

They walked slowly, reading the little signs to each other. The path was full of gentle curves, and more than once they surprised squirrels and rabbits on the path. Jessie watched a squirrel retreat swiftly up the trunk of a tree, and that was when she noticed that the sky was no longer blue. A cool breeze swept through the woods, and the branches overhead shivered.

"Cold front moving through," Toni said importantly. "That means it's probably going to rain."

Jessie stopped. Without intending to, she glanced over her shoulder. "Shouldn't we go back then?" she asked uneasily. "We'll get soaked."

"What if we do?" Toni held a finger to her lips. "Listen, you can hear the rain coming. It sounds like little feet — millions of 'em." She looked excited at the idea, and when the first drops began to fall, she raised her face and laughed.

"Come on," she urged. "Let's run. We can wait on the schoolhouse porch till it passes." She darted ahead, moving quickly in spite of her crippled foot. Jessie started to follow before the impact of the words hit her. Then she skidded to a halt, almost falling on a root that crossed the path.

"Wait *where*?"

Toni turned around and stared. "What's the matter with you? I said we can wait on the schoolhouse porch. It's just a little way from here."

"What schoolhouse?" Jessie could hardly say the words. "What are you talking about?"

Toni looked annoyed. "It's an old schoolhouse the McNaughtons bought when the county was going to tear it down. They moved it onto the preserve to fix it up, but they never got around to it.

24

It's been locked up ever since." She frowned. "Come *on*, Jessie. What's wrong?"

The rain was beating down now, and the wind pressed Jessie's wet T-shirt and shorts against her skin. "We shouldn't go there," she said weakly. "It's — it's private property."

"That's just silly," Toni snapped. "You can walk all the way back in the rain if you want, but not me." She started to run again and vanished almost at once around the next turn in the path.

Jessie hesitated. She could go back alone, but the path behind her looked spooky, more like a tunnel than a path.

"Wait for me," she shouted. The wind swallowed her words. "Toni, wait for me."

CHAPTER FOUR

It was the schoolhouse of her dreams. The peeling white paint, the little bell tower, the empty flower boxes, each detail was exactly as Jessie had seen it.

"Hurry up!" Toni shouted. "What are you waiting for?" She was halfway across the clearing, her face glistening with raindrops, her eyes shining. Jessie's stomach lurched, and she felt as if she were going to be sick. Reluctantly, she moved out from the trees. Spikes of grass clung to her legs, and the rain stung her cheeks. She followed Toni up onto the little porch and leaned against the railing.

"We should have gone b-back." Jessie's lips were stiff. "We're going to get just as wet here as we would have on the trail."

"You're right," Toni agreed. She grasped the doorknob with both hands and pulled.

"No, don't!" Jessie tried to drag her away. "We can't go in there."

"What's the matter with you?" Toni demanded. "Nobody would expect us to stay out on the porch if we can go inside and keep dry. We're not going to hurt anything — "

She broke off as the door creaked open.

"You see, it wasn't even locked!" Toni exclaimed triumphantly. "Come on."

"It should have been locked," Jessie protested. "You said it was always locked."

She might as well have been talking to herself. Toni stepped through the doorway, almost tripping on the uneven sill. There was nothing to do but follow her.

I wish this was another dream so I could wake up! Jess thought frantically. But this time the schoolhouse was real.

They were standing near the front of a large classroom. Rows of desks, small ones near the front, larger ones toward the back, faced a teacher's desk that was mounted on a low platform. Dusty chalkboards covered the front wall.

"It *is* kind of spooky," Toni admitted. She seemed a little less sure of herself now.

The wind slammed the door behind them, and both girls jumped. In spite of the rain pattering on the roof and streaking the windows, the rest of the world seemed far away.

"Look, there's a door in the back of the room." Toni pointed. "Want to see where it goes?"

Jessie took a step backward. "You can if you want. I'm staying here."

She didn't care if she sounded like a coward. There was no way she could explain how frightened she was. She'd felt threatened in her nightmares, but finding herself inside the schoolhouse was a thousand times worse. She was absolutely certain that terrible danger lurked in the shadowy corners of this room or crouched behind the desks.

"I don't see what you're worried about." Toni sounded impatient, but there was a tense note in her voice, too. If she was scared, she was trying hard to cover it up. The more Jessie hung back, the more determined her companion would be to prove she wasn't afraid of *anything*.

Jessie watched while Toni made her way between the rows of desks to the back of the classroom and peered through the doorway.

"There's a little hallway here with a door at each end. Bathrooms, I guess. And another door straight ahead." Toni disappeared briefly and there was the sound of a door opening, then a scream.

"What is it?" Jessie wailed.

Toni reappeared, her face pale in the half dark. "A mouse!" she exclaimed. "I opened the door — it's a closet — and a mouse ran out. Yuk!" She started back up the aisle and stumbled again, catching herself on a desk.

Jessie darted forward, then stopped at the expression on Toni's face.

"I'm okay! There's a loose board back here."

She moved more slowly now, wincing with each step. Jessie looked away.

Something lay on the floor under one of the desks. It was curled in a half circle and trembled a little, almost as if it were alive. Jessie edged around the desk for a closer look. She bent, then leaped back in horror.

"Now what's wrong?" Toni demanded irritably. "Hey, where are you going?"

Jessie didn't answer. She was through the schoolhouse door, down the steps, and part way across the clearing before she could make herself stop and look back. Toni was just limping through the door.

"What's the matter, Jessie? Did you see the mouse, too?"

Jessie shook her head wordlessly. She waited for Toni to catch up, and they hurried toward the trail.

"If it wasn't a mouse, what was it?" Toni persisted. "A spider? Spiders won't hurt you — most of them, anyway."

Jessie looked straight ahead. Raindrops trickled inside her shirt collar and blurred her vision.

"Was it a rat?" Toni asked, watching her curiously. "I wouldn't blame you for running if you saw a rat."

"It was nothing," Jessie snapped. "I just want to get away from here, okay?"

They hurried on. Jessie longed to run, but she knew Toni's foot was hurting. It would be cruel to race ahead. But we don't have to talk, she thought grimly. And she can stop asking questions because I'm not going to answer.

There was no way on earth she would admit that what had sent her running out into the rain was a pale-blue hair ribbon.

CHAPTER FIVE

For the next two days, Jessie stayed inside and tried not to think about the schoolhouse. The hike back to the parking lot had seemed endless, and Toni had had to stop several times to rest her foot during the bike ride home. With each stop she had scowled more fiercely. Jessie tried once to break the silence, apologizing for running away, but by that time Toni was unreachable.

"Forget it!" Maybe it was the pain in her foot, and maybe it was disgust at the way the hike had ended. In any case, her tone made it clear that there wasn't anything Jessie Belland could do or say that interested her in the least.

It wouldn't be so bad, Jessie admitted ruefully, if she hadn't practically begged Toni to go with her to the nature preserve. And for a while it had been fun, with Toni obviously enjoying the role of guide. But the schoolhouse had changed everything. Now they'd probably never be friends.

Depressed and scared, Jessie wandered around the house, unable to settle down. Sunlight streamed through the windows, streaking the pale-green carpets and making the antique tables glow. She ran her fingers over the satiny wood, studied the paintings and photographs, played the music boxes scattered through the house. Finally she went up to her bedroom, where Grandma's portrait smiled down at her.

What would her grandmother say if she knew what was happening? *Don't give up, Jessie. We Bellands can handle our problems.* She wondered if her grandmother had ever had a nightmare come true.

"You look just the way she did then." Her father was at the door, his eyes on the portrait. "The likeness is pretty amazing."

Jessie perched cross-legged on the bed in front of the portrait. "I don't *feel* like her," she said glumly. "At least, I don't think Grandma Belland ever felt the way I do."

"How's that? Are you homesick?"

Jessie shook her head. "I'm — " She started to say "scared" but changed it to "sad." If she said she was scared she'd have to explain, and her dad might try to laugh away her fear. "I really messed up with Toni Draves. I don't think we're ever going to be friends."

He walked around the bed for a closer look at the portrait. "I'm sure your grandma found some people hard to know when she was growing up," he said. "She probably still does, but she's learned how to handle it. You'll learn, too."

Jessie shrugged. "Maybe."

"Anyway," he went on, "things never go as smoothly as you hope they will. I'm certainly finding that out."

She looked up, startled at his tone.

"You mean, like writing the book?" she asked. "I guess that's hard, too."

"You bet it is," he said soberly. "I've been thinking about doing this ever since I came back from Vietnam, but I guess I never really believed it would happen. Now I have the chance and I'm not sure — you see, I have to remember a lot of things that I'd rather forget." He rubbed his jaw. "Yeah, it's hard."

So her father was scared, too. Like her, he was up against something he'd never experienced before. But it was different with grown-ups, Jessie thought wistfully. They had problems, but they always seemed able to figure a way out. She couldn't see any way out of hers. A creepy schoolhouse and a couple of bad dreams were spoiling the perfect summer she'd looked forward to when Grandma Belland invited them to move into her house.

"Well, back to work." Mr. Belland sighed. "I'm going to get through the first chapter this week if it kills me. Maybe getting started is the hardest part. What are you going to do?"

"Work on my tan." Jessie didn't care much about lying in the sun, but she couldn't say she just wanted to stretch out on the bed and feel sorry for herself.

"Good idea."

They walked downstairs together, and Jessie watched her father settle himself in front of the typewriter out on the porch. Then she went into the dining room and out through the French doors to the little side garden. An arc of lilac bushes formed a wall around the lounge that stood in the center of the lawn. Jessie was sure this must be one of Grandma Belland's favorite spots. The semicircle of green was like an outdoor room, private, yet open to birds and butterflies, the scent of flowers, and glittering blue sky overhead.

She settled herself on the lounge and closed her eyes. She didn't expect to fall asleep, but her grandmother seemed very close in this quiet spot, and the thought was comforting. Maybe she was letting herself get upset about something that really didn't matter. If you dreamed every night, surely sooner or later a dream was bound to come true. And the blue ribbon — that could have been left behind by a hiker who had visited the school-house long ago. . . .

She woke shivering. When she opened her eyes, she saw that a wind was whipping the topmost branches of the lilac bushes. She sat up, hugging herself against the chill, and looked around.

The woman in the blue dress was standing right behind her. The blonde hair was held back by a blue headband, and her smooth features were twisted into an expression of such loathing that Jessie cried out in terror.

"Dad!"

A fierce gust of wind swept through the garden, and the woman faded into the swaying branches of the lilacs. Jessie scrambled to her feet and threw open the French doors just as her father catapulted around the corner into the dining room.

"Jessie, for Pete's sake — "

She pointed through the door. "Someone was there! A woman! She was standing right next to me!"

Her father dashed outside and looked around wildly. When he returned, his face was white and set.

"Were you asleep out there?"

"I — I guess so." Jessie couldn't stop shaking.

"Then you dreamed the woman," her father said bluntly. "There's no way an intruder could get through those bushes." He pulled a chair away from the table and sat down with a thump.

"I didn't dream her!" Jessie exclaimed. "I didn't! She was standing right there. And I've seen her before, Dad — " She stopped, because her father wasn't listening. He rubbed his eyes tiredly.

"When you yelled," he said, "I was making myself remember a day in 'Nam when six of us went into a village that had just been shelled. Most of the huts were burning, and the people — " He shook his head. "I felt as if I were back there, living through it all over again while I wrote about it. Then you called, and for a minute it was as if you were there, too." He looked up wonderingly. "You weren't even born yet, but you were there. That was the worst of all, imagining *you* in that terrible place."

Jessie didn't know what to say. She felt as if her father was talking to himself.

"I really did see her, Dad," she repeated. "I was so scared. . . ."

Her father stood up. "Looks like we're both having bad dreams," he said wearily. "But I'll tell you one thing, Jess, I'd rather have your dreams than mine." He gave her a quick hug and headed back to the porch.

Jessie stared into the garden. She'd never be able to go out there again without being afraid. Day by day, a ghost in a blue dress was spoiling everything, and Jessie didn't know what to do.

She certainly couldn't tell her father.

CHAPTER SIX

Mrs. Belland shifted the casserole to the front of the oven and dipped a spoon into it.

"Pretty blah," she commented, after a quick taste. "Are you sure you added the salt, Jessie?"

Jessie groaned. "I put in everything the recipe said. It's not my fault if — "

"Oh, for heaven's sake," her mother gestured impatiently. "Don't start arguing. Salt or no salt — what's one more disaster!"

"I'm tired of casseroles anyway," Jessie grumbled. She looked out the window, not wanting her mother to see how close she was to tears. "I'm going to watch television."

"Set the table first, please." Mrs. Belland's voice softened suddenly. "On the porch, if you like. It's nice out there."

Jessie opened the silverware drawer and began counting out knives, forks, and spoons. "What else happened today?" she asked after a moment. "I mean, what other disasters?"

Her mother made a face. "Nothing happened,"

she said. "That's the trouble. I am simply bored to death with my job, that's all. A year ago I was in charge of a whole office, and I was good at it. Now I just stand around the store trying to be helpful and failing miserably. It's making me crabby."

Jessie felt sorry for her mother but resentful, too. Everybody else talks about their troubles, but no one listens to mine, she thought crossly. Her father had dismissed what happened today as a bad dream, and Jessie didn't even consider mentioning the woman in the garden to her mother. "Supernatural nonsense," was what her mother would say. "Life has enough *real* problems."

One person who would listen — Jessie was sure of it — was Grandma Belland. She had always been interested in what Jessie had to say. She might even have an explanation for the nightmares and the appearance of the woman in blue. If Grandma Belland were to walk in right now . . . Jessie's heart lifted at the thought.

"Come on in here," Jessie's father shouted from the front of the house. "It's your grandmother!"

Jessie gasped and flew down the hall to the front door.

"No — in here," her father called from the den. "Hurry up or you'll miss her!"

Jessie hurtled into the den with her mother right behind her. There, looking out at them from the television screen, was Grandma Belland. There was no mistaking the cap of curly, graying hair, the glowing pink cheeks, the brown eyes sparkling with enthusiasm.

"She's giving a speech to a conference of middle-school principals," Mr. Belland whispered. "How about that!"

They listened for a moment, and then the news report moved on to another story. Jessie felt lost as the picture changed to a view of the White House in Washington. For a moment Grandma Belland had seemed to be right there with them.

"My mother the public speaker," Mr. Belland said proudly. He switched off the television. "Just think — here's a lady who went to a little one-room schoolhouse till she finished eighth grade and now she's giving advice to the principals of schools with hundreds of students."

Jessie sat down. "Do you mean Grandma went to that little school in the nature preserve?"

"Of course she did. Only it was out on the highway then. She grew up in this house, and that was the only grade school close by. By the time I was born, she and Grandpa Belland had already bought a house in Willow, and I went to school there. She taught for years at the county high school in town, but I think she always liked country living best. That's why she moved back here after Grandpa died."

So Grandma Belland knew all about the schoolhouse. More than ever, Jessie wished she could confide in her grandmother.

"Maybe we could call and tell her we saw her on television," Jessie suggested. "And we could ask her when she can come for a visit."

Mrs. Belland turned back toward the kitchen with a sigh. "I'm sure she's much too busy to come right now," she said. "When you have an exciting job like that, you don't want to leave it. I hope she knows how lucky she is."

Left alone, Jessie and her father stared at each other. "We'll call your grandma in a day or two," Mr. Belland said after a moment. "Even if she can't come for a visit right now, it might help to talk to her, right?"

Jessie was pretty sure he meant it might help him, too. "Right," she said quickly. "Let's do it."

She was in the clearing again. It was early evening; the setting sun shed an eerie red light through the circle of trees. Jessie knew what was going to happen. In a minute the door of the schoolhouse would open, and the woman in the blue dress would come out. This time I'll run, Jessie promised herself. But when the woman appeared, her face a pale mask of hatred, the blue eyes held Jessie like a magnet. She couldn't run, couldn't scream. And this time the woman moved more swiftly, down the schoolhouse steps and across the clearing. In a moment they would be face-to-face and it would be too late. . . .

Too late for what? Jessie sat up in bed, clutching the sheet. Awake, she was as terrified as she'd been when she was dreaming. Her fingers fumbled for the bedside lamp, and when she found the switch at last she looked around the room in panic, expecting to see the woman in blue glaring at her. The feeling of being watched was very strong, just as it had been in the garden.

She slid out of bed, snatched up a pillow and blanket, and tiptoed down the hallway past her parents' bedroom, to the spare room at the end of the hall. Maybe changing rooms would help, maybe not, but she couldn't stay where she was. If she didn't do something, she would lie awake, afraid to close her eyes, for the rest of the night.

41

CHAPTER SEVEN

"I can't imagine why you'd rather sleep in that little box of a room than in your grandmother's bedroom," Mrs. Belland said the next morning. "It's obviously been used as a storeroom for years. I'll bet the mattress sags."

"It's okay," Jessie said. "I just want to try it for a while."

Her mother raised her eyebrows but didn't ask any more questions. "You'd better make a fresh pot of coffee after I leave," she said. "Your father was up at five this morning — I could hear the typewriter rattling away."

It wasn't rattling now. They listened for a moment, and then Mrs. Belland picked up her handbag from the counter and headed toward the door to the garage. "See you at the usual time," she said with a sigh. "There's a note on the refrigerator telling you what to do to start supper."

Jessie finished her toast and cereal and stacked the dishes in the dishwasher. Then she rinsed out the leftovers in the coffeepot and started a fresh pot perking. She thought about telling her father the coffee would be ready soon, but a peek through the porch door changed her mind. He was hunched over the typewriter with his chin resting on his fists, scowling into space. Better not to interrupt, she decided, and tiptoed upstairs.

Her mother was right. The mattress in the little bedroom was lumpy, with a deep dent in the middle. There were suitcases stacked in a corner of the room and the only furniture besides the bed was a chest of drawers and a rather battered rocking chair. But Jessie had slept soundly on the lumpy mattress. Perhaps, she thought, the woman in the blue dress haunted only special places — Grandma Belland's bedroom, the little side garden.

She pulled out the dresser drawers. Boxes and folders of business papers, all neatly labeled, filled the top two. The next two were empty. There was plenty of room for her clothes, if she decided to move them into the little room. She tried the bottom drawer and found it, too, was empty, except for a gray box tied with string and labeled: *Diaries, Eileen Yates.*

Eileen Yates. That had been Grandma Belland's name before she was married. If her diaries were in the box, they would tell about events that had happened a long time ago. Maybe, things that had happened in the little schoolhouse. . . .

Jessie picked up the box, then dropped it. She had kept a diary herself once, a red leather book that she'd received for her tenth birthday. For a couple of months she'd written in it every night. Then one day she'd made the mistake of taking it to school, and Billy Claypool had stolen it from her bookbag. During recess he'd read it out loud, while Jessie, red-faced and furious, hid in the girls' restroom. Eventually her teacher had rescued the book and returned it, but Jessie had never written in it again.

Diaries were supposed to be private.

Of course, she argued with herself, it wouldn't do any harm to open the box just to see if there were really diaries inside.

She untied the string and lifted the cover. Inside were two books that looked much like the diary Jessie had been given. Beneath them lay a spiral-bound notebook. She picked up one of the little diaries. If she looked inside, would Grandma be as angry with her as Jessie herself had been with Billy Claypool?

But this really is different, she told herself. I wouldn't be reading it to be mean. I'd do it because I'm scared, and the diaries might help me understand what's happening. Grandma would want to help me if she knew. . . .

When you really and truly wanted to do something, it was pretty easy to talk yourself into it. Jessie flipped open the little diary to the first page.

The date, January 1, 1933, was printed in the left-hand corner. She figured rapidly and decided Grandma would have been nine years old then. Below the date, Eileen Yates had written in pencil:

My New Year's Resolutions

1. Ride my bike faster than Sandra.
2. Do my homework before I listen to the radio.
3. Learn to tap-dance like Shirley Temple.
4. Brush my teeth even if Mom forgets to tell me.
5. Never tell a lie unless I can't help it.

Jessie grinned. The list of resolutions sounded a lot like lists she had made up herself. She turned the page, eager to read more about Eileen. But the next page was blank, and so was the one after that. It wasn't until January fifteenth that there was another entry.

I'm going to be just like Miss Caldwell when I grow up. She's so pretty. Marion calls her the Queen of Hearts because of her ring.

45

On the page for January sixteenth there were three words printed in capital letters: BIG ARITHMETIC TEST!

After that the diary was blank until the twenty-sixth of May, when there was another heading in capitals:

NEWS BULLETIN! Eileen Yates starred in the Spring Play and everyone said she was very good. Miss Caldwell said it the most.

And that was all. With growing disappointment Jessie flipped the pages of the diary. They were all blank, until she reached December 31. Grandma Eileen must have remembered her neglected book then and decided to write in it one last time. The two sentences were written so large that they filled the page.

I HOPE AUNT EMILY DOESN'T SEND ME ANY MORE DIARIES. I'D RATHER DO THINGS THAN WRITE ABOUT THEM!!!!!

She picked up the second little book and opened it. The date was 1932, a year earlier than the other book, and the childish writing was so smudged and uneven that Jessie could hardly read it.

Aunt Emily sent me this book for Christmas. I'm supposed to write stuff in it. I don't want to.

That was the only entry in the diary. Grandma Belland must have saved it all these years, because that single, stubborn little message made her laugh. It made Jessie laugh, too.

Still, it would have been nice if her grandmother had enjoyed keeping a diary. Even if the books never mentioned the schoolhouse, Jessie knew she would have liked reading whatever Eileen Yates had to say.

The black-and-white, spiral-bound notebook at the bottom of the box had HOMEWORK ASSIGNMENTS lettered in bright red across the cover. Jessie flipped it open without much interest.

A carefully drawn skull glared up at her from the first page. Under the drawing were two words: KEEP OUT!

She turned the page again and found a drawing of a dagger with bright-red drops raining from its tip onto the letters below: PRIVATE!

The third page had no picture, but the lettering was so big that it crowded the edges of the paper: THIS MEANS YOU!

What a fuss over a list of homework assignments! Jessie looked up guiltily, half expecting to

47

find someone watching her from the doorway —
her father, perhaps, or her grandmother magically
transported from Madison to scold a nosy granddaughter. Or the woman in the blue dress. But no
one was there.

She turned another page and began to read.

CHAPTER EIGHT

January 16, 1937

Miss Caldwell wants us to keep journals during the last semester of eighth grade. We don't have to write every single night, though, and we can let her read them or not, whatever we want. Marion and Sandra say they are going to let Miss C. read what they write, because she might give them extra credit, but I'm not. I'll probably write some really secret stuff I wouldn't want anyone else to read, ever. ESPECIALLY Miss Caldwell!

Joe and Timmy Boyer are boiling mad. They say they have nothing to write about except the weather and which pig had a litter and how many eggs they collected that morning. And since they are twins and do everything together, their journals will be exactly the same. I think that's silly. Even twins must have some secrets!

I have a special reason for never showing my journal to Miss Caldwell. She is the one I'll probably write about the most. She's been my ideal person ever since she came to Willow Township

School when I was in third grade. And now she is going to live right here in our house until school lets out! She was staying with the Johnsons, but they sold their farm and so she has to move out by February 1. Three different families have offered her a room, but she picked us.

I can hardly wait for her to move in. She's going to have the room at the end of the hall. It is very little, but she says she doesn't care at all, because the view of the fields and hills is so pretty.

I don't think it was the view that made her choose us, though. It might be Uncle Peter. He is Mom's younger brother, and he just moved back here from Colorado. He's working at the Kreuger farm now and living there, too. Uncle Peter and Miss C. danced together four times at Ann Johnson's wedding, and he has offered to help move her things to our house. Maybe they will fall in love and get married. If they do, I'll probably be in the wedding because Uncle Peter is my godfather as well as my uncle. Sandra and Marion will *hate* me! They are pretty jealous already, because Miss C. is going to live with us. Marion says she definitely wouldn't want a teacher in her house watching everything she did.

January 25

It's really fun being in the eighth grade, even if there are only five of us. We get to help with the younger kids and Miss C. lets me correct the third-grade arithmetic papers when I finish my own work. I think I'm going to be a teacher some day — *if* I can have pretty clothes and gorgeous blonde hair like hers.

February 2

Miss Caldwell moved in yesterday. Uncle Peter helped carry her things upstairs, and Mom invited him to stay for dinner. He said the pork roast was good but the company was even better. He looked at Miss C. when he said that.

Miss C. says she feels lucky to be staying at our house, and she knows she's going to enjoy being part of our family. I thought that was nice, but Mom looked kind of worried when she said it. Later I heard her telling Miss Caldwell that Uncle Peter has always been a great one for the ladies, but he moves around a lot. Miss Caldwell said he was the most charming man she'd ever met.

February 16

We got back our essays on winter today, and I got an A-plus. Sandra got an A-minus, and Marion got a B. Joe and Timmy both got C's. Miss Caldwell read my essay out loud and said it was lovely. Some of the little kids clapped, but Marion and Sandra didn't, and the boys pretended to fall asleep. On the way home Sandra said it was an okay essay

51

but hers was just as good. She said I'd better watch out because nobody likes a teacher's pet.

I'm *not* a teacher's pet! Can I help it if Miss C. thought my essay was better than anyone else's?

February 19

Today was Miss Caldwell's birthday. Mom made cupcakes for her to take to school, and we had a party instead of outdoor recess in the afternoon. It was too cold to go out, anyway. Miss C. said she was twenty-seven years old, and she made each of us tell what we hoped we would be doing when we are twenty-seven. Most of the little kids said they want to be firemen or clowns or president of the United States. Joe and Timmy are going to be farmers like their dad. Marion wants to have six children, three boys and three girls. I said I want to be a teacher and get married, too. Or else I will be the editor of the *Willow Weekly News* like my father. Sandra said she wants to be famous.

Miss C.'s cupcake had a candle on it. She made a wish, but she wouldn't tell us what it was.

February 20

We had ELEVEN INCHES OF SNOW last night! We all stayed home, even Dad. He said the paper will just have to be a day late this week. We couldn't open the back door because the snow had drifted so high, so Dad climbed out through the kitchen window and shoveled a clear space. Then we sprinkled about a bushel of crumbs and seeds for the poor birds.

It was strange being inside all day. I finished my new Nancy Drew mystery and read an old one over again. Mom made cookies, and Miss C. walked around smiling and humming to herself. She's wearing her birthday present from Uncle Peter. It's a beautiful gold heart with a smaller heart inside. It matches the gold-heart ring her folks gave her when she graduated from high school. I heard Mom tell Dad that Uncle Peter better be careful or he would break somebody's heart. Dad said it was none of our business.

March 16

Last night I tried an experiment. Sandra and Marion say Miss Caldwell always gives me the best marks because she's in love with Uncle Peter and she wants to please him. I told them Uncle Peter doesn't care about my marks — Mom says he never did a lick of work in school — but they won't listen. Today they wouldn't even sit with me at lunch.

About the experiment. We were supposed to write a report about the best book we've read all year. Sandra picked *Little Women* and Marion chose *Treasure Island*. They know Miss Caldwell likes those books. So I wrote about *Nancy Drew and the Circle of Gold*. Miss C. always says Nancy

Drew is fine for fun, but she thinks we should read other kinds of books most of the time. She'll probably give me a D or an F, and Sandra and Marion will be sorry they've been so DISGUSTING!

March 21

We got our book reports back this morning. Sandra and Marion both got B's. Miss Caldwell wrote on my paper, "I wish you had chosen a more challenging book, but your comments about the story and characters are extremely interesting." She gave me an A.

I tried to hide my mark, but Joe peeked over my shoulder, and he told the others. Sandra's face got all red. She wouldn't even look at me on the way home from school.

I told Mom, and she said if Miss C. favors me I should just do the best work I can and try not to listen to S. and M. She says it's silly to *try* to get a low grade for any reason. And she also said she thinks Uncle Peter is going to be moving on pretty soon. She says he's never stayed in one place very long and she doubts if he ever will. I guess she thinks Marion and Sandra are right. But it's still not my fault!

The doorbell rang, and Jessie jumped. From the moment she'd opened "Homework Assignments," she'd been living in another world. Dazed, she laid the notebook on the bed and hurried down the hall, her mind filled with what Eileen had written.

She was at the top of the stairs when her father came out of the kitchen, a handful of papers in one hand and a coffee cup in the other.

"Oh, there you are, Jess," he said. "Good. You can go to the door. Looks as if it's someone for you, anyway."

"For me?" Jessie ducked her head to see through the glass in the front door. To her astonishment, Toni Draves was standing on the porch.

CHAPTER NINE

"You can have this if you want it." Toni thrust a booklet at Jessie. "The McNaughtons had it printed to tell about the flowers and trees on their property. It mentions the schoolhouse, too." She cocked her head, daring Jessie to say she wasn't interested in the schoolhouse.

"Thanks." Jessie led the way into the living room. "I'm sorry I — I sort of ran out on you the other day. That school is a spooky place."

"It doesn't matter." Toni managed to sound as if she were used to people running away without a reason.

"This house is really pretty," she went on, unexpectedly. "You're lucky."

"It's not our house," Jessie explained. "We're just staying here while my grandma's in Madison."

Toni wandered around the room, examining the piano, the painting over the fireplace, the bouquet of dried flowers on the coffee table. "Your grandmother always waved when she drove by me on the road," she said. "She wasn't snooty like most people. . . . Is your other house as nice as this one?"

"We don't have a house in St. Louis. We were living in an apartment before we came here. My folks put our stuff in storage." Jessie felt as if she were being tested.

"Is that your dad typing out there?" Toni nodded toward the door opening onto the side porch. "What's he doing?"

"He's writing a book," Jessie said proudly. Then she wondered if that sounded like bragging.

But Toni just nodded respectfully. "I always wanted to see the inside of this house," she admitted, sitting down at last. "Ever since we moved here from Iowa when I was eight. We drove down the road and I saw this house up on the hill, and I thought, Oh, good! that's it. But then we turned in next door instead. I thought at first we were going to live in the barn. I couldn't see the house back there beyond the trees so I thought . . ." She shrugged the memory away.

"Do you like living on a farm?"

Toni looked bored. "It's all right. The farm belonged to my grandfather. He left it to my mom when he died, but then she died, too, when I was seven. We were living in Iowa then, and my dad decided to move back here. So that's what we did."

"Maybe your grandma and mine went to school together when they were kids," Jessie suggested cautiously. "I found my grandma's diary, and she wrote about two girls — Marion and Sandra. There were only five people in her class, and the other two were boys, Joe and Timmy Boyer."

"The Boyer farm is about three miles down the highway," Toni said. "I think two brothers own it." She didn't sound particularly interested.

"But your grandma," Jessie persisted. "Could she have been Sandra or Marion?"

Toni shook her head. "My grandma's name was Sophie — and that's all I know about her, so it's no use asking. My dad never talks much about the family — or anything else," she added sourly. "The only time we talk is when he's telling me to cheer up and think about what a good time I'm going to have in school next year. That's a joke! He'll find out."

"Find out what?" Jessie asked, forgetting caution.

"That I'm not going back to school! I'm going to say my foot hurts too much, and they'll have to let me have a tutor at home. There was a boy in our class who was hurt in a tractor accident last year, and now he has a tutor at home. That's what I want."

Jessie was shocked. "But you'll be all by yourself," she protested. "You won't have any fun."

Toni looked disgusted. "Do you call school fun?" she demanded. "I can have a much better time by myself. A great time!"

"They won't let you stay home," Jessie argued. "They'll know you can walk and run and ride your bike and — and everything. People can't just stay home because they want to."

Toni stood up and limped over to the piano. "Then I'll run away," she said in a low voice, her back to Jessie. "I can do that. Wait and see."

The typewriter on the porch had fallen silent. Jessie wondered if her father was overhearing this conversation and was as stunned by it as she was. She had always liked school herself. As for running away — that was something she'd never even thought about. The idea chilled her.

"Anyway," Toni said and turned around abruptly, "I came over here to ask you something. It's very important."

Jessie held her breath. If Toni wanted a friend to run away with her, she'd have to look somewhere else.

"Are you a cat person?"

The unexpectedness of the question made Jessie blink. "I — I don't know," she said. "I've never had a cat."

"Then you're not," Toni said firmly. She seemed to be thinking over what to say next. "See, my cat Barney Mae had four kittens a few days ago, and I thought maybe you'd like one of them. You can't have it right away — the babies are too young. But you could come over and pick out the one you want."

"Oh, neat!" Jessie was relieved and thrilled. A kitten would be wonderful. "I'll have to ask my folks, but I'm pretty sure they'll say yes. I could never have a pet when we were living in apartments."

"Well, then." Toni pressed a piano key so gently that it made no sound. "Will you come tomorrow?"

"Okay. If you're sure you want to give one away."

"Of course I want to," Toni said tartly. "We don't need five cats. The more I can give away the better. Maybe you can take two."

She left then, limping out the front door and down the walk to the road where she'd left her bike. Jessie stood at the door, ready to wave goodbye, but Toni didn't look back.

When she went back into the house, she found her father in the living room.

"I was eavesdropping," he said. "Hope you don't mind."

"That's okay."

"Actually, it would have been pretty hard *not* to hear," her father went on. "That's one angry young lady."

"She says the kids at school don't want to be friends — I guess because she's lame," Jessie said. "She really hates school."

"That was pretty obvious." Mr. Belland dropped into a chair and stretched his long legs. "Remember Heather Streatham?" he asked suddenly.

Jessie looked at her father in surprise. Heather had lived two floors below them in the apartment-before-the-last-one, and they had been in the fourth grade together. She walked with a crutch and had worn a neck brace, the results of a car accident.

"Toni's *nothing* like Heather," Jessie protested. "Heather liked everybody. She was always smiling."

Her father nodded. "Always," he agreed. "And she was almost always alone. I used to see her walking to school. She must have had to get up before dawn to get there on time."

"She wasn't always alone, I walked with her sometimes," Jessie said defensively. "Part of the way, at least." She shifted from one foot to the other, remembering many other times when she'd shouted a "Hi!" to Heather and scooted right past to catch up with friends at the corner. "She didn't expect everyone to walk as slowly as she had to."

"No, I don't suppose she did," her father said. "But people handle their problems in different ways. I'll bet sometimes Heather resented being left behind. She was just a lot more careful about showing it."

Jessie rolled her eyes and kept still.

"Anyway, Toni is trying," her father said. "Coming over here like that — offering you a kitten."

"I think she wanted to see Grandma Belland's house," Jessie said. "That's probably the real reason she came."

Her father shrugged. "I wouldn't bet on it. Do you want the kitten?"

"Oh, yes!" Jessie was glad to change the subject. "Do you think Mom will care?"

"I don't know." Her father's smile faded, and a moment later he stood up, stretched, and headed back to the porch. "See what kind of day she's had before you ask," he advised. "And make it one kitten, not two. Your mom is more like Toni than Heather when it comes to showing her feelings. She lets it all hang out."

Left alone again, Jessie wandered back upstairs to the little room at the end of the hall. A half hour ago she had resented the sound of the doorbell that had interrupted her reading of Grandma Belland's journal. Now she felt too muddled and confused to concentrate.

The notebook labeled "Homework Assignments" lay on the bed where she'd left it. Jessie picked it up and thumbed the pages. Maybe she could find a description of Miss Caldwell. *Pretty — blonde hair* — that was all. So far, the *evidence* suggested that the teacher could be the woman in the blue dress, but there was no way to be sure.

And if it *was* Miss Caldwell, why was the ghost

so angry? That was the biggest question. Jessie thought about what her father had said: People handle their problems in different ways. They smiled like Heather Streatham. They snapped and snarled like Toni. Was it possible — she shivered — that maybe sometimes they got so angry that their anger continued after death?

CHAPTER TEN

April 19, 1937

Last night Miss Caldwell and Uncle Peter went to Willow to see a movie in the high-school gym. She told us about it at breakfast. This man and his girlfriend were going to get married, but then he got sick, and he broke their engagement so she wouldn't have to watch him fade away and die. After he left, she stabbed herself with a silver letter opener!

Miss Caldwell said it was a beautiful story and she cried through the whole thing. I asked Mom if we could go to see it this weekend, but she said it didn't sound like her cup of tea. She said a woman should always remember that when God closes a door he usually opens a window, so there's no reason to go looking for a letter opener!

I *think* she was trying to warn Miss Caldwell about Uncle Peter again, but I don't think Miss C. even noticed. She wears her heart pendant every single day, and when Uncle Peter stops in she fusses over him and laughs and laughs.

April 22

Today was the most exciting day of 1937 — so far! First Miss Caldwell said she had an announcement for the eighth grade. Then she read us a letter from the Cooper Academy for Girls in Madison. They are offering a scholarship to "an outstanding eighth-grade rural female living in central Wisconsin." They have a test they will send to any school that asks for it, and all the rural females who want to will take the test on the same day — May 23rd. Their teachers will send the test papers back to the Academy, and a judge will pick the winner.

When Miss C. finished reading the letter, I had the queerest feeling that it was written to ME. I'm a rural eighth-grade female living in central Wisconsin. I get good grades. And I would just LOVE to go to Cooper! Miss Caldwell said the winner will be very lucky, because Cooper also gives college scholarships to some of its graduates. And girls who go to Cooper live on the campus and go to plays and concerts in Madison and have wonderful times.

I can hardly wait for May 23rd. If you really, really want something, I believe you can make it happen!

April 23

Big fight with Sandra today. She is mean! We were eating our lunch on the front steps, and I just happened to say that I'd really like to win the scholarship. And Marion said she'd like to win it, too, but if she did she might be afraid to go away to school. She said she guessed Willow High School would be okay with her. Sandra didn't say anything at first, but then her face got red, and all of a sudden she was SHOUTING. She said Willow High wasn't okay with her, and she wanted to win the scholarship more than anything in the world but she knew she didn't have a chance. I said, What do you mean? and she said, You know what I mean. And then SHE THREW A PICKLE AT ME!

We started screaming at each other, and I was just going to throw my apple core at her when Miss Caldwell ran out on the porch and told us to stop acting like babies. She said the Cooper Academy wouldn't be interested in girls who yelled and threw things. She said she was ashamed of us. That made me feel like crying, but I didn't.

Sandra looked as mad as anything all the rest of the day, and when school was over she ran ahead so she could walk by herself. Marion and I walked together, but she only said one thing all the way home. She said maybe it would be best if she was the person who won the scholarship, because she was the kind of girl who never threw things at anybody.

April 24

I thought Miss C. would tell Mom and Dad about what happened at school yesterday, but so far she hasn't. She did tell them about the scholarship test, though, and Dad is as excited as I am. He says going to Cooper would be a great experience, but he could never afford to send me there himself. Mom said I better not think too much about winning, because there will be other girls who want to win as much as I do.

I don't think anyone *could* want it as much as I do — unless it's Sandra. She wouldn't look at me all day. Marion says Sandra thinks Miss Caldwell will figure out a way to make sure my test paper is the best one from our school. I told her Miss C. wouldn't cheat, but I think Marion believes it, too. Marion says Miss C. is in love with Uncle Peter and everyone knows it. She says when you're in love with a person, you'll do anything to please him.

May 4

I haven't written in my journal for a while because I haven't felt like it. Sandra has been awful — calls me teacher's pet and little princess and silly names like that whenever Miss Caldwell isn't around. Most of the time Marion eats lunch with her and I eat by myself, but today Miss C. called all three of us to her desk after lunch and told us it was time to patch up our quarrel — "whatever the reason" — and be friends again. If she only knew!

Anyway, maybe school will be better now. Sandra didn't run ahead this afternoon, and she and Marion and I walked home together. We didn't talk about the scholarship test at all, even though I can hardly think about anything else.

Miss Caldwell expects to get copies of the test soon, and we will take it on Saturday morning at school. She will be in charge, and she'll send our papers to Madison to be judged. When she told us that, I could feel Sandra glaring at me, and I knew what she was thinking. But she's wrong! Miss Caldwell isn't a cheater and neither am I. (Even though I'll just die if I don't win.)

May 9

Something horrible happened tonight! Uncle Peter stopped in and Mom invited him to stay for dinner (that isn't the horrible part). He came out into the kitchen while I was setting the table, and he said I was turning into a pretty young lady, which was nice but doesn't mean anything because that's just the way he talks. Then he said, in an offhand sort of way, that he'd about decided to move to California in June.

You should have heard Mom! She wanted to know right away if he'd told Miss Caldwell his plans, and he said no, he hadn't gotten around to it yet, what was the hurry? Mom said it was wicked to be so indifferent to other people's feelings, and then she stormed into the living room to tell Dad. She tried to keep her voice down, but we both heard her say Peter was moving and he hadn't bothered to tell Miss Caldwell, and what were they going to do about it? And Dad said they weren't going to do anything because it was none of our business.

Right in the middle of all that, Miss Caldwell sailed out of her bedroom with a new dress on and a ribbon around her hair. Her face was all pink and shiny, and even though she pretended to be surprised to see Uncle Peter we knew she'd probably heard him drive up. And maybe she'd heard all the rest, too.

Miss Caldwell and I did most of the talking at dinner, because Mom and Dad weren't speaking to each other, and Uncle Peter was sulking. Afterward he and Miss C. went out on the front porch and sat on the swing. Mom muttered to herself all the time she washed the dishes and I wiped. I could hardly wait to go up to my bedroom.

It's not my fault that my windows were open and one of them is right above the porch. I didn't try to listen, but I heard anyway. Uncle Peter must have already told Miss C. about moving to California. She was saying it was just wonderful, but she didn't sound as if she meant it. And then she said she'd always thought she'd like California herself, and she certainly didn't intend to spend her whole life in the Midwest without ever trying anyplace else. When he didn't say anything, she began to tell him how much she would miss him and how she had enjoyed all their time together and she had thought they really understood each other.

It was pretty mushy and embarrassing! I should have gone back downstairs right then. Mom says eavesdroppers usually hear something they'd rather not know, and she's right. Because all of a sudden I heard Miss C. say something about Eileen, so naturally I kept on listening. She said she was very fond of me and wanted the best for me, and she knew Uncle Peter felt the same way. And then she said this awful thing. She said, "I'm in a position to guarantee that Eileen will do better than anyone else on the scholarship test."

For a second or two I was really happy when she said that, because I thought she meant I was smart enough to beat everyone else. But then I thought about her words again, and how she'd said them, and about how they would sound to Sandra and Marion if they'd been there listening with me. I could just hear them yelling "I told you so, I told you so," all over the place, and I guess I wouldn't blame them.

If only the test weren't so important!

CHAPTER ELEVEN

"For heaven's sake, you haven't done that since you were five years old." Mrs. Belland eyed the milk-filled trench that divided Jessie's oatmeal into two equal parts. "Eat your cereal while it's warm, Jess — don't play with it."

Jessie mashed her spoon into the middle of the trench and watched the milk fill up the hole. She had been listening for her father's footsteps in the upstairs hall, but she guessed he was still sleeping. He'd been up and down all night, her mother said, unable to fall asleep until nearly morning.

Jessie had been restless, too. She couldn't remember her dreams, but she knew the events in Grandma Belland's diary had been part of them. This morning she'd read the last entry again, and then she'd searched the bottom drawer of the dresser, in vain, for another notebook. She had to find out what had happened after Eileen's "horrible evening." The long-ago scholarship test might have nothing to do with the mystery of the woman in blue, but Jessie couldn't stop wondering.

"We'll have chicken tonight," Mrs. Belland said briskly. "It's in a baking dish ready to go. All you have to do is heat the oven and put it in at five."

Jessie nodded. She wondered if this would be a good time to ask about the kitten. Last night had definitely not been a good time; her mother had come home from work in a worse mood than usual.

"This customer had to have number-ten nails," she'd reported crossly, as they ate their dinner. "And when I said we were out of them he threw a tantrum. Acted as if it was all my fault! I wanted to tell him he was lucky if this was the first time that had happened to him. We're *always* running out of things. And the clerks just have to stand there and take the blame! I've told Mr. Andersen he needs to put everything on a computer, so he can keep track of what he needs, but he doesn't pay any attention."

Jessie had glanced sideways at her father, who was listening with a pained expression. She could guess his thoughts: Her mother had to put up with a job she hated so that he could write his book. That meant it was his fault she had to listen to customers' tantrums.

"What are you going to do today?"

Her mother's question brought Jessie back to the present. "I'm going over to see Toni. She has some kittens, and she said I could have one of them if you said it was okay. They aren't old enough to

73

leave their mother yet, but later . . ."

She paused, waiting for an explosion that didn't come. "I suppose a kitten would be fun for you," Mrs. Belland said. She reached into the refrigerator for her brown-bag lunch. "Until we move back to St. Louis, that is. We're not going to be here forever, you know." The thought seemed to please her, and she gave Jessie a quick hug before hurrying to the door. "Have a good time with your friend," she added. "And tell Dad I hope the writing goes well today."

Nearly an hour passed before Mr. Belland came downstairs, yawning noisily. He looked pleased when Jessie gave him her mother's message.

"She's having a hard time of it," he said. "Did you ask her about the kitten?"

"It's okay." Jessie put some bread into the toaster while he poured a cup of coffee. She waited until he'd taken his first sip before she asked the question uppermost in her mind.

"Do you know if Grandma Belland won a scholarship when she was in eighth grade? Did she go to the Cooper Academy in Madison, or did she go to the high school in Willow?"

Her father ran his fingers through his already mussed-up hair. "She went to Cooper — I've heard her talk often enough about how much she liked it there. But did she have a scholarship? She may have. Cooper is an expensive school. My grand-

74

parents believed in getting all the education you could, but they weren't rich." He raised his eyebrows at Jessie. "Why do you want to know?"

Jessie explained about the notebook labeled "Homework Assignments." "It's all about what happened to Grandma in eighth grade," she explained. "Do you think she'll be angry when she finds out I read her private book?"

"I doubt it." Her father grinned. "There's not much *you* could do that would make her angry."

"The trouble is, she wrote a lot about a scholarship test and how important it was going to be, but then the journal ends. Wouldn't you think she'd have started a new one and kept writing?"

"She probably did. Maybe the next book was lost, or maybe she just got tired of writing in it and threw it away. Next time we talk to her on the phone you can ask her what happened."

Jessie sighed. She was remembering what Eileen's mother had said about eavesdropping: You usually found out things you would rather not have known. Reading someone else's diary was just as bad. Jessie wished she'd never heard about the scholarship test, because now it wouldn't be enough to know whether Grandma had won or not. Jessie had to know what part, if any, Miss Caldwell had played in the winning.

While her father ate his breakfast, she went

back upstairs and opened the diary again to the last page.

If only the test weren't so important! Jessie bit her lip. What exactly had Eileen been thinking when she wrote that?

Toni was waiting at the mailbox when Jessie turned in at the Draves' gravel road an hour later.

"What did your folks say?" she demanded, before Jessie was off her bike. "Can you have a kitten?"

Jessie nodded. She rested the bike against a tree and followed Toni up the road.

"How about two of them? They'd be company for each other."

"Just one," Jessie said. "But you know what? This will be the first pet I've had in my entire life!"

When Toni smiled she looked like a different person. Her dark eyes shone. "Once you have a cat you'll be a cat person forever," she announced. "Wait and see." Unexpectedly, she turned up the ramp that led into the barn. "Barney had her kittens out here," she explained. "And when we took them into the house she got upset and carried them back. We'll try it again when they're older — if we haven't given them all away by then."

The inside of the barn was dim and fragrant. Toni pointed to a ladder halfway down the aisle that divided the two rows of empty stalls. "You'll have to go up in the loft to see them," she said. "My dad moved them up there so they wouldn't get trampled when the cows come in for milking. They like it up there," she added. "There's lots of mice for Barney Mae to chase when she isn't taking care of the babies."

Jessie looked at the tall ladder. "You're coming up, too, aren't you?" she asked. "You can help me choose."

Too late, she realized it was the wrong thing to say. Toni's smile faded.

"I have to put some clothes in the washing machine," she said gruffly. "I'll be back in a few minutes. Go ahead and pick out the kitten you want, but you have to leave it here for a couple of weeks."

She limped out of the barn, leaving Jessie to stare after her in dismay. *How could I be so dumb?* she wondered. She was a little nervous about the ladder herself, and climbing must be a hundred times harder for Toni. *But I didn't mean to hurt her feelings!* It would be nice if, just once, they could meet without Toni getting angry or acting hurt.

The ladder stretched up into a rectangle of dusty light. Jessie climbed slowly, careful not to look down. When she neared the opening, the mewing grew louder, and Barney Mae appeared, looking down at her visitor with interest.

"Good cat." Jessie put out a hand, then hastily gripped the ladder once more. "Good kitty. . . ."

Barney's eyes widened. She shrank back out of reach.

"Hey, where are you going?" Jessie climbed one more rung, raising her head through the opening. Bars of sunlight stretched down from an opening in the front of the barn and from tiny windows on either side. Where they met, a few feet in front of the opening, the woman in blue stood as straight and still as a statue.

Jessie tried to cry out, but no sound came from her mouth. Then the woman moved. Gliding forward, she gripped the top of the ladder and began to shake it.

"Don't!" Jessie managed a scream as the ladder swung back and forth, threatening to tip her off. The woman bent closer, her eyes glittering.

"Please!" Jessie screamed, louder this time. She began to slip down the ladder, fingers clenched, her toes barely touching the rungs. Halfway down, a wrenching shake sent her hurtling to the floor below. The last thing she saw was the woman's terrible smile and the flash of a heart-shaped pendant on a chain.

CHAPTER TWELVE

"Here, girl, are you okay?"

Jessie opened her eyes and stared at the red-faced man bending over her. He looked as frightened as she was. Above him loomed the opening to the loft, empty now, except for the ladder.

"I — I don't know." She pushed herself up on her elbows, wiggled her toes. One shoulder hurt a little and her head throbbed. She peered into the stalls on either side, afraid of what might be lurking in the shadows of the barn.

"Are you Jessie Belland?"

Jessie nodded and let the man help her to her feet. "I'm Frank Draves — Toni's dad. She said you might be comin' over this morning to pick out a kitten. What happened? Did you lose your balance on the ladder?"

Jessie didn't answer.

"I guess city kids don't do much climbin'," Mr. Draves went on. "Glad you're not hurt — that could have been a nasty fall if you'd hit the edge of a stall. Guess I should have brought the litter down so you could look at 'em."

"I didn't just fall," Jessie protested. "I mean, I didn't slip."

"Didn't, huh?" Mr. Draves pushed his cap to the back of his head. "First I hear you yellin', and then I find you lying on your back on a pile of straw. If you didn't slip, what were you up to?"

"I wasn't up to anything," Jessie said, with as much dignity as she could manage. "Someone tried to knock me off the ladder. Honestly, Mr. Draves. It was rocking back and forth so hard, I couldn't hold on."

"Are you sayin' someone's up there?" He looked at her in astonishment. "That's crazy, unless there's a tramp. . . ." He turned suddenly and started up the ladder, moving swiftly in spite of his size. "You go outside," he shouted over his shoulder.

Jessie walked shakily to the door of the barn. Why had she tried to explain what had happened? It would have been better to let Toni's father think she had simply lost her balance. There was no one in the hayloft — not now. The woman in the blue dress would be gone, just as she'd vanished when Jessie's father had run outside looking for her in the garden.

"Hey, what's going on?" Toni appeared around the corner of the barn. "You've got straw in your hair. What happened?"

Before Jessie could reply, Mr. Draves joined them.

"Your friend thought she saw somebody up there in the loft," he explained, puffing. "Says the person knocked her off the ladder on purpose." He watched Jessie warily, as if he wondered what odd thing she'd say next. "There's no one up there now, I can tell you that." He mopped his sunburned face and grinned. "Must have been a ghost."

"Like at the schoolhouse that day," Toni said after a moment. "You thought you saw a ghost there, too, didn't you?"

"I did not!" Jessie's face burned. "I never said I saw a ghost. I just said it was a sort of spooky place."

"Same thing." Toni shrugged. "You sure ran."

Mr. Draves patted Jessie's shoulder. "It don't matter," he said. "As long as you didn't hurt yourself. Come on up the road and rest — I've got something to show you, and you might as well sit down while you're lookin'. You're still sort of green around the gills."

He led the way down the ramp and along the road with the two girls close behind, not looking at each other. When they reached the spruce trees, he crouched and began emptying his overall pockets.

"Two orange ones, a gray one, and a gray-and-white," he announced, lining up four tiny kittens on the grass. "Now you sit a while and decide which one you want. I've got to get back to work. If you want a ride home later, you let me know."

Jessie thanked him and dropped to her knees on the grass, facing the barn. She was still shaking, but she hoped it didn't show.

"You don't have to be scared out here," Toni said sweetly. "The big bad ghost can't get you now."

Jessie glared at her.

"The orange kittens are the cutest, I think," Toni said, after a long silence. "They look like Barney Mae."

Jessie stroked a tiny orange head with one finger, and the kitten promptly turned away from its playmates to sniff her knees. "They're all cute," she said softly. "This one is perfect." She lifted the kitten and cuddled it, wincing as pinprick claws dug into her shirt. "Is it a boy or a girl?"

"A boy." Toni picked up the gray-and-white. "Listen, Jessie, did you really think you saw a ghost? What did it look like?"

Jessie unhooked the kitten's claws from her

shirt and put the tiny creature back with its family. "Never mind," she said. "You wouldn't believe me anyway."

"Well, if *I* saw a ghost, I wouldn't be scared," Toni said. "I'd think it was exciting."

Jessie stood up hastily. "You wouldn't say that if it tried to kill you. I have to go home. Do we just leave the kittens here, or what?"

"My dad'll put them back." Toni couldn't resist another question. "What do you mean, a ghost tried to kill you? You're making that up, right?"

Jessie shook her head. As she turned to leave, Barney Mae came down the ramp from the barn and started across the grass toward her family. If only cats could talk, Jessie thought. Barney was up there in the loft. She knows what happened.

But cats couldn't talk, so Toni would go on thinking Jessie was a superstitious baby, and Mr. Draves would go on thinking that city girls didn't know how to climb ladders. For the first time in Jessie's life, someone — or something — had actually tried to hurt her, and no one believed her.

It was a relief to get away from the Draves' barn and Toni's questions. At least, Jessie thought, as she biked along the highway and up the drive to Grandma Belland's house, she no longer had to wonder who the woman in blue was. Every detail of those terrifying moments on the ladder was burned into her memory — especially the sight of the heart-within-a-heart pendant that swung from the woman's neck. It was Uncle Peter's gift — the one Miss Caldwell had treasured. Something terrible had changed Eileen's teacher from a happy, loving person to a murderous phantom.

Jessie could think of only one person who might know what had happened.

"I want to call Grandma," she announced after dinner that evening. "We ought to tell her we saw her on television."

"Good idea," her father agreed. He sounded tired, and so did her mother. Neither of them had talked much during dinner, though they'd listened and smiled when she described the orange kitten.

"Just don't talk too long," Mrs. Belland warned. "We can't afford a big telephone bill."

Jessie followed her father into the den and waited while he found Grandma's Madison telephone number.

"You first," he said. "I'll give your mom a hand in the kitchen, and you call me when you're through talking."

Jessie's fingers trembled as she tapped out the

number. It had been a long afternoon. Her shoulder had continued to hurt, but worse than that, she'd been afraid to go outside alone, or even upstairs. Settled, finally, with a book in the living room, her father working close by on the porch, it had been the thought of making this call that had kept her from panicking.

"Jessie, is that you? Oh, how wonderful! How's my family? Are you enjoying being a country girl?"

Relief flooded through Jessie at the sound of her grandmother's voice. "I'm — we're okay, Grandma. I love your house. And we saw you on television."

"Oh, that." Her grandmother chuckled. "I would have called you but I didn't know they were going to tape it." She paused. "Is everything all right, dear? You sound kind of tense."

In a rush of words Jessie told about meeting Toni Draves and about the orange kitten. "We went for a hike one day, but most of the time I just stay around the house." She took a deep breath. "I read a lot. I even read your diaries, Grandma. I found them in a box in the dresser, and I thought maybe you wouldn't mind since they were so old."

Her grandmother laughed. "Old is right!" she said. "They go all the way back to grade school."

"Is it okay that I read them? I know they were supposed to be private. The eighth-grade one, anyway."

Her grandmother stopped laughing. "Of course it's okay," she said, but suddenly Jessie wasn't sure she meant it.

"I liked reading about your little school and everything," she said timidly. "The teacher — Miss Caldwell — she must have been really pretty."

Now there was no mistaking Grandma's hesitation. "Oh, she was pretty, all right," she said slowly. "But it was all a very long time ago, Jessie. When I left eighth grade my whole life changed. I went away to school in Madison, and a new world opened up for me. I don't look back very much."

"I guess you won the scholarship then?" Jessie clutched the telephone so tightly that her fingers ached.

"Yes. Yes, I did. How is your dad's writing coming along, dear?"

Jessie blinked. As surely as if Grandma Belland had said the words, she had served notice that the subject of the scholarship was closed.

"I'll — I'll call Dad," she said hastily. "He wants to talk to you, too. I miss you, Grandma. I wish you could come to see us." She put the phone down fast, not wanting to hear a reply. If her grandmother said she was too busy to come, it might be because of the nosy questions Jessie had asked.

When she'd called her father to the phone, Jessie went into the living room and threw herself on the couch. I should have told her everything, she thought. I should have told her Mom is grumpy and Dad is worried about his book and I'm scared to death. Things couldn't get much worse than that unless — unless it turned out Grandma was hiding something — something bad. And that was exactly the way she'd sounded.

CHAPTER
THIRTEEN

If only she could find another journal! Without much hope, Jessie pulled out one dresser drawer after another, then turned to the closet of the little bedroom. A box on the floor contained neat bundles of cancelled checks. Jessie closed it quickly. A carton of shoes stood next to it. There was nothing else. The overhead shelf was empty except for a couple of hats in plastic boxes.

I'm not just being nosy, she told herself, when she climbed into bed at last. (She could imagine what her mother would say if she'd seen her looking into that box of checks.) I'm scared! I'm scared of the dark, being alone, everything! She switched off the bedside lamp and promptly turned it on again.

When she finally fell asleep, another nightmare was waiting.

She was back at the schoolhouse, standing on the little porch and looking through the open doorway. The schoolroom was full of shadows, but she could see the teacher's desk quite clearly, and the first row of students' desks. A musty odor of chalk and old books tickled her nose.

She stood still, trying to remember why she had come. She'd been looking for something important, and the search had brought her to the school.

She stepped into the shadows. At once, there was a stirring in the overheated air, and the door slammed shut behind her. Darkness covered her eyes like a blindfold. She tried to take a deep breath, but her chest felt tight. Panic-stricken, she struggled to find the doorknob.

A hand closed on her shoulder.

Jessie fought wildly for a moment, before she realized she was in bed, her face buried in the pillow. Gasping, she rolled over and looked around. The room was empty, and very still except for the white curtains lifting in the breeze. She took big gulps of fresh air, then slipped out of bed and tiptoed into the hall. A glow at the top of the stairs and the smell of toast told her she wasn't the only one awake.

Mr. Belland looked up from his coffee mug when she padded into the kitchen.

"Well, well, another night stalker. What got you up at two in the morning?"

Jessie slid into the breakfast nook beside him.

"Bad dream," she muttered.

"Again? What was it about?"

"I was in a dark place and I couldn't breathe and something grabbed me." Jessie shivered, reliving that last second or two before she'd wakened. "I've had dreams sort of like it before. In the other bedroom."

"So that's why you moved." He nodded. "I guess a change of setting is a good idea sometimes. It didn't work tonight, huh? Sorry."

Jessie curled up on the bench and hugged her knees. "Did you have a bad dream, too?"

"Nope. I'm just not getting much sleep the last few nights." He hesitated and then seemed to make up his mind about something. "To tell you the truth, Jess, the change of setting hasn't done much for me either. I'm beginning to wonder if we made a mistake moving out here. Your mom's sure unhappy, and I'm afraid I don't have what it takes to write a book. Unfortunately."

"But you've been writing all week," Jessie protested. "I've heard you."

Her father nodded. "I've got quite a bit down on paper," he agreed. "But back in St. Louis I thought I knew just how to do it. I'd describe what happened in Vietnam to me and my friends — how we felt about it — and then tell about our support groups and how they work. Trouble is, I'm having trouble putting it all together. The parts I've written are like pieces in a jigsaw puzzle — they won't mean much if I can't put them together in one big picture. Do you understand?"

Jessie didn't.

"The thing is," he continued, "I wonder if I should give up the book idea right now. Maybe we should head back to the city and start job-hunting again. Your mom would like that — what do *you* think?"

Yes! Jessie felt featherlight, as if, in a single sentence, her father had solved all her problems. This was what she wanted, wasn't it? To get away from this house and the school and the questions she'd never be able to answer?

"If that's what you want — " she began.

"It was dumb of me to think I could just sit down at the typewriter and that would be all there was to it. How stupid can you be?" He grinned, but his eyes were sad. He looked the way he had back in St. Louis, when day after day of job-hunting had failed to produce results. For the last few weeks — ever since they had decided to accept Grandma Belland's offer to live in her house while she was away — the look had been gone. Jessie hated to see it return. She reached over and gave him a hug.

"Well, what do you think?" he asked again. "Are you ready to start packing? This hasn't been such a great week for you either, has it? Bad dreams, nobody to do things with except that sulky kid next door. . . ."

Jessie wanted to shout, "Let's leave tomorrow!" Still, the expression in her dad's eyes told her that what she said next was important. If he gave up the book now, the sad look might be there forever.

"I'd just as soon stay for a while," she fibbed. "Writing a book takes a lot of time, doesn't it? I bet you can do it. We haven't been here very long."

She held her breath, hoping he'd argue. Instead he smiled, as if he'd heard what he wanted to hear.

"You don't just look like your grandmother, Jess," he said thoughtfully. "You think like her, too. When we called her last night, I told her what I was feeling, and she said exactly what you just said. You're a great pair of cheerleaders. I just hope I can give you something to cheer about."

"You will." Jessie sighed. She was glad that she sounded like her grandmother and sorry they were going to stay.

"Time for us night owls to turn in," her father said. "I've got work to do tomorrow, right?"

"Right."

She waited while he put his cup in the sink and switched off the kitchen light. Then they tiptoed up the stairs together.

"No more bad dreams, Jess — sleep well." The whispered words followed her to the little room at the end of the hall where the bedside lamp still burned. She slid under the covers and closed her eyes, trying to hold on to the gratitude she'd heard in her father's voice.

She had said the right thing.

They were going to stay.

They wouldn't give up.

Then her left hand, tucked under the pillow, closed around a scrap of something smooth. When she pulled it out into the lamplight, a length of blue ribbon dangled close to her eyes.

CHAPTER FOURTEEN

"I don't know why I came back here today!" Jessie exclaimed. "I should have known you wouldn't believe me. But yesterday you kept asking about the ghost, and I though maybe if I showed you the ribbon . . . oh, well! I just wanted to talk to *somebody* about it."

That had been her first thought when she got out of bed this morning. Since she'd convinced her father they should stay a while longer in Grandma Belland's house, she was going to have to figure out a way to make the stay bearable.

Toni shrugged. "It looks like an ordinary blue ribbon to me. Nice color," she added slyly.

They were sitting on the lawn in front of the spruce trees again, watching Mr. Draves trudge up the slope from the barn. Toni had listened without comment as Jessie described her nightmares and the terrifying appearances of the woman in the blue dress. Now she looped the ribbon around her finger and held it up to the sun.

"Well, it *isn't* an ordinary ribbon," Jessie snapped. "I never had a ribbon like that, so how did it get under my pillow?"

"Don't ask me." Toni grinned. "When I asked you what the ghost looked like, I just wanted to see what you'd say. Nobody *really* believes in ghosts."

Jessie bit back a retort as Mr. Draves joined them. "Thought you might like another look at Barney's family," he said cheerfully. "I decided I'd better bring 'em down this time — don't want you up on that ladder again." He laid the kittens at Jessie's feet and grinned down at her. "You feeling better today? No cuts or bruises?"

"I'm okay." Jessie's head ached but she was pretty sure that was the result of the long night just past, rather than yesterday's fall. "Thanks for bringing the kittens."

"No problem." He looked at Toni anxiously and then started back toward the barn. "You come again any time," he called to Jessie, over his shoulder. "Toni can use some company."

"I hate it when he does that," Toni growled. "He acts as if I'm five years old and need a little friend to play with. He's always fussing — thinks I can't do anything myself."

"What are you talking about?" Jessie was astonished. "All he said was — "

95

"I know what he said." Toni yanked a handful of grass from the earth and sprinkled the fragments over the kittens, much to their delight. "He likes *you*, of course," she added jealously. "He likes people who smile a lot. He wants people to smile even if they don't have anything to smile about."

"Well, he probably thinks I'm crazy," Jessie said. "I shouldn't have told him someone pushed me off the ladder. I *knew* she wouldn't be there when he looked."

Toni began to gather up the kittens. "Oh, don't worry about that," she said. "He just thinks you have a lively imagination." She imitated her father's deep voice.

"I didn't imagine this ribbon, did I?" Jessie demanded. "It was under my pillow! And I saw another ribbon just like it that day we were in the schoolhouse. It was lying on the floor — that was why I ran away."

For a moment Toni looked uncertain. Then she shook her head. "I don't believe there's any such thing as a ghost," she said. "Sorry. You can believe in 'em if you want, but not me."

Jessie stood up. "Okay," she said tiredly. "I was thinking though, maybe since my grandmother went to the schoolhouse, it seems like your grandmother must have, too. Are you sure she didn't?"

"I told you, I don't know anything about her.

Anyway, I don't see what she has to do with your ghost. If you want to find out more about the school, you ought to go back there and look around again." Toni slanted a grin in Jessie's direction. "I'll go with you — unless you're too scared, that is."

"No, thanks." Jessie gave her kitten a last pat and started down toward the road, moving more quickly as she passed the open door of the barn. Telling Toni her problems had been a really dumb idea. Toni Draves didn't want to hear about any problems but her own.

"Why in the world don't you just go to bed?" Mrs. Belland peered at Jessie over the top of her reading glasses. "You've dozed off a half-dozen times in the last hour."

Jessie blinked, trying to focus on the television screen, and then gave up. "I guess I *am* pretty tired," she admitted. She glanced uneasily at the dark window across from her, then at the doorway leading to the hall and the stairs. "Are you going to bed soon?"

"We won't be long." Her father looked at her sympathetically. "Why?"

"I just wondered." Jessie avoided his eyes. "I think I'll move back to Grandma's room tonight." She'd decided that afternoon that there wasn't any point in staying in the little bedroom, since the woman in blue, and the nightmares, followed wherever she went.

"Why don't you leave your door open," Mr. Belland suggested. "Let the air circulate."

"Okay." Jessie knew her father was thinking about her bad dreams, and she was grateful. It helped to know he would be there if she called, but it didn't take away the fear.

What am I going to do? she asked herself, for the hundredth time that day. If she had to, she could tell her dad what she'd told Toni this morning, but it would only upset him when he already had a lot on his mind. As for her mother, in a million years she couldn't imagine her mother, well — even if she'd been there in the Draves' barn, even if she'd seen the ghost-woman reach down and shake the ladder, her mother wouldn't believe what had happened.

If only Grandma Belland were here! The telephone conversation had raised more questions in Jessie's mind than it had answered, and she hadn't even had a chance to tell Grandma why she was so interested in the journal. If Grandma knew about the dreams, and about the way the woman in the blue dress had tried to hurt her, and about the hair ribbons . . .

Jessie sat up. "I'm going to write a letter," she announced. Maybe Grandma wouldn't be able to provide answers, but she wouldn't jeer, like Toni, and she wouldn't say the ghost was in Jessie's imagination. Writing down the whole weird business might help — unless, of course, Grandma wrote back and told Jessie something she didn't want to hear. Something awful about exactly how Eileen Yates, not Marion or Sandra, had won the scholarship to the Cooper Academy.

CHAPTER FIFTEEN

"It was sweet of you to write to your grand-mother, Jessie." Mrs. Belland sounded unusually cheerful at breakfast the next morning. "She'll be glad to hear from you. If you want, I'll take the letter to town with me so it'll be sure to go out today."

Jessie looked at the envelope propped on the kitchen counter. She wasn't sure Grandma Belland would be pleased with the contents, but writing the letter had helped. Afterward, she had fallen asleep quickly and hadn't awakened until the telephone rang around seven.

"Maybe your grandma will be able to get back here for a visit soon," Mr. Belland suggested. "Seems to me we could all use some more of her pep talks."

"I told her that," Jessie said, and they grinned at each other.

Mrs. Belland took a last sip of coffee and pushed back her chair. "I'm going in early today," she announced. "Mr. Andersen called and said he had something he wanted to talk about. That's all he said," she added, before they could ask. She hurried around the table and gave each of them a hug. Then she scooped up her handbag and Jessie's letter. "Have a good day, you two."

"Good luck," Jessie said automatically, but her mother had already gone, letting the screen door slam behind her.

"Could mean trouble," Mr. Belland commented. "Maybe the store is laying people off."

"But Mom sounded kind of excited," Jessie pointed out. "She wouldn't sound like that if she thought she was going to be laid off, would she?"

"Hard to say." The worry-crease was back in her father's forehead. "She's not exactly crazy about that job, you know."

They listened to the sound of the Chevy backing down the slope to the road and buzzing off toward town. Jessie crossed her fingers and toes. Make it something good, she prayed.

The mystery was solved an hour later. Jessie was in the living room reading, and her father was working on the porch, when the telephone rang. The sound, slicing through the stillness, made Jessie bite down hard on a fingernail.

"Jess, guess what!" Her mother's voice was a lilting whisper. "I can't talk long on Mr. Andersen's phone, but I wanted to call you and Dad right away.

101

It looks as if I have a new job! Something I can really get my teeth into!"

"At the hardware store?" Jessie realized she'd been holding her breath.

"Remember, I told you how we're always running out of things? Well, it turns out Mr. Andersen wouldn't talk about keeping track with a computer because he's scared to death of the whole idea. Doesn't know the first thing about computers. I told him I'd been working with them for years, but he acted as if he couldn't care less. Well! Today he said he'd thought it over and he wants me to find out how much it would cost to do what I suggested. And if we do it, I'll be in charge of the whole project!"

Jessie couldn't remember when she'd heard her mother sound so happy. "That's terrific!" she exclaimed. "I'll call Dad."

"No, don't. I can't tie up the phone any longer. You just repeat what I told you, okay?" There was a click at the other end of the line.

Jessie hurried out to the deck.

"GOOD!" her father shouted when she'd given him the news. He pushed the typewriter away and leaned back with a sigh. "Your mom's an amazing woman, Jessie my girl." He shook his head wonderingly. "What a reee-lief!"

That's what it was, Jessie thought — a reee-lief! Something good had happened at last.

The thought stayed with her, a little candle of hope, for the rest of the day. In the middle of the afternoon Mr. Belland announced that he was quitting work early, and together they baked a two-layer cake, using a recipe from Grandma Belland's collection. The finished cake sloped a little, and the chocolate frosting had a few lumps, but Jessie was pleased with it anyway.

"We could put a candle on it," she suggested. "So Mom will know it's special."

"She'll know." Mr. Belland had a smudge of chocolate on one cheek and another streak on his chin. "Want to help clean out the frosting bowl? The grill is lit for the hamburgers, so we might as well relax till the guest of honor comes home."

They took the bowl out onto the porch and settled down to wait. Looking out at the garden and the fields beyond, Jessie thought about how happy she'd been to come here. If only . . .

"Want to ask Toni to join us for hamburgers?" Mr. Belland asked suddenly. "Maybe it would cheer her up a little."

Jessie shook her head. "I think she's mad at me again. When I was there yesterday, she said her dad liked me because I smiled a lot."

"So?"

"It made her angry. I guess she doesn't think she has anything to smile about."

Her father handed her the mixing spoon half

103

filled with frosting and proceeded to clean out the bowl with a rubber scraper. "That kid's sure handicapped," he said. "In more ways than one. Some of the people I'm writing about are a lot like her. They lost an arm or a leg in the war, and that was a terrible thing. Trouble is, that was a long time ago, and what's missing is still more important to them than what's left. I know other people who were just as badly hurt, but they've managed to keep going and have good lives."

He broke off as the blue Chevy turned onto the road and started toward them. Halfway up the slope, the horn blasted a triumphant *toot-a-toot*. It was so unlike her usually no-nonsense mother that Jessie and her father laughed out loud.

Nothing more was said about calling Toni. Still, Jessie felt a twinge of guilt as she crossed the yard to meet her mother. It was that talk about war veterans, she decided. It would be very easy to think about what was lost instead of what was left.

The celebration was a huge success. Mrs. Belland said that the hamburgers were the best she'd ever tasted and the cake was beautiful. By the time they'd had their supper on the porch and cleaned up afterward, Jessie felt more relaxed than she had for days.

"Jess, do me a favor." Her mother was on the porch, enjoying the last glimmering light, while her father hovered over his typewriter, squinting down at the sheet of paper still in the machine. "Will you go in and find the Madison directory for me? I think I saw one in the bottom desk drawer in the living room. I want to look over the computer firms that have the kind of equipment we'll need. I'm going to work early again tomorrow and place some calls before the store opens."

The desk was close to the sliding doors, and the Madison telephone book was where her mother had said it would be, stored on top of a stack of magazines. Jessie lifted it out and was about to close the drawer when she froze. The edge of a familiar black-and-white cover was sticking out from beneath the magazines.

"Is it there, Jess?"

Her mother's voice seemed far away. With trembling fingers Jessie pulled out the notebook. "Homework Assignments" was lettered across the front, in green this time.

"Jess?"

"I'm coming."

She flipped the notebook open. There were no scary pictures or warnings in this one, and only a few pages had been filled with Eileen's neat handwriting. The date at the top of the first page was May 11.

So there had been another journal, just as she'd suspected. But why was it down here in the living room? Why hadn't it been packed away with the others? Jessie's heart pounded with excitement and dread as she dropped the notebook back in the drawer and hurried out to the deck. Reading the notebook would have to wait, but not for long. Before she went to sleep tonight, she would know what had happened in that long-ago May.

CHAPTER SIXTEEN

May 11

I wish we'd have a tornado! That's a terrible way to start my new journal, but I don't mean the kind of tornado that knocks down barns and hurts people. I'd just like a little private one that would pick me up and carry me away for a while. Like Dorothy in *The Wizard of Oz*.

Things started going wrong as soon as I woke up this morning. Miss Caldwell usually goes to school early, and I stay upstairs till she's ready to leave. That's so *people* won't see me walking with her and say I'm trying to be her pal or something. I stay in bed till I hear her go downstairs, and then I get dressed while she's eating breakfast. But this morning she didn't get up until late, and then she stayed in the bathroom such a long time that I fell asleep again. When I did finally get up (Mom called me and was *cross*), first I broke a shoelace and then I couldn't find my silver fountain pen that Uncle Peter gave me for Christmas. (It was under the bed — I must have dropped it when I finished writing in my journal Saturday night.)

Miss Caldwell was gone when I finally got downstairs, and Mom and Dad were out on the porch. Mom was asking him if he noticed that Miss C.'s eyes were all red and puffy, and then she said she's sorry they ever invited Miss C. to live with us. She said it had brought nothing but heartache, and she wished Uncle Peter had had a few more spankings when he was a boy.

Right in the middle of all that, she must have remembered I might be listening, because she came flying back into the kitchen and practically pushed me out of the house. She said I was going to be late for sure, and she was right. The worst thing about that was that I could have walked to school with Miss C. today and nobody would have cared. Marion and Sandra are both home with the flu!

Mom was right about Miss Caldwell's eyes, too. And she was probably right about the heartache, if heartache makes a person cranky. Miss C. scolded every single student at least once, including me. I know I shouldn't have been late, but she never made a big thing about it before. I wished Sandra and Marion had been there to hear her. They wouldn't have dared call me teacher's pet after that!

At noon I ate lunch by myself, and then I turned rope for some of the little girls who wanted to jump. It was boring but better than sitting on the porch feeling sorry for myself.

In the afternoon we had a surprise history quiz, and Miss C. said Sandra and Marion would just have to make it up when they recovered. She sounded as if she thought they might be faking, but Marion's little brother said she'd been throwing up all night, so I don't think Miss C. was being fair. Then she scolded me again, because my test paper was full of blots, and that wasn't fair either. I think the point of my pen cracked when it fell on the floor Saturday. Any other day she would have told me to switch to a pencil and keep going, but today she made me copy the whole test over.

May 12

I know I promised to write in this journal till the middle of May, but I'm beginning to hate it. There's nothing to write about but school, and with Miss C. so crabby, I'm beginning to hate school, too. The trouble is, we have to show her our journals in about a week, so she can see how many pages we've filled. We get a grade for effort, even if we don't let her read what we've written.

Miss C. didn't eat dinner with us tonight. She

said she wasn't hungry. Maybe she's coming down with the flu, but I don't think so.

May 13

Sandra and Marion are back in school. They look so pale and puny that I think even Miss C. feels sorry for them. Today I was sorry for *her*, because she wasn't crabby anymore, just quiet and sad. When Timmy Boyer fell asleep during math, she didn't even notice. Marion and Sandra giggled about the way she was acting, and Sandra whispered something about "unlucky in love." I suppose that means everybody knows Uncle Peter is moving to California.

May 15

Two days of flu! I've been so sick, I haven't even felt like reading. Mom made me stay in my room so I wouldn't expose Miss Caldwell to my germs and make the whole school sick. As if Marion and Sandra hadn't already done it!

Dad brought the radio upstairs, and I listened to some serials this afternoon. Mostly, though, I just daydreamed about going to Cooper Academy next year. I can't help it — I think about going all the time. Mom says it's silly to count on something that probably won't happen, but Dad says I have a good head on my shoulders so I've got a better-than-some chance of winning the scholarship. I told him Marion and Sandra think I'm going to win, too, but I didn't tell him why.

May 16

Still feel sickish this morning.

Mom has said about a dozen times that she wasn't going to invite Uncle Peter for dinner again before he left for California because he ought to understand that seeing him would make Miss C. feel bad. But I was pretty sure she couldn't hold out. Sure enough, at breakfast this morning she said she'd asked him to come for dinner tonight, since he liked fried chicken and that happened to be what she was fixing. She tried to sound as if his coming was so unimportant that she'd almost forgotten to mention it. I was watching Miss C., and it sure wasn't unimportant to her. First she turned kind of pink. Then, quick as a wink, she said it was too bad she was going to see Ann Johnson Hunt's new house this evening, and would we please give Peter her best wishes for a good trip. And *then* she rushed upstairs to her bedroom and closed the door.

That got Mom started all over again. She was just saying she hoped she'd live to see the day when Uncle Peter settled down — when all of a sudden we heard Miss C.'s steps on the stairs, and she came rushing down. There were two bright spots on her cheeks and eyes were shining. "I just remembered it's *next* Saturday I go to Ann's," she said. "How could I make a silly mistake like that!" And back up to her room she went again.

I thought Mom would be pleased, but all she said was, "Well, I warned her. Some girls never learn!" And then she *ordered* me to lie down and rest so I'd be sure to feel better by tonight. She said she expected me to sit at the table and talk, even if I couldn't eat a thing, since it would take all of us to keep the conversation going.

She worried all afternoon about what was going to happen. You could tell by the way she banged the pots around in the kitchen. Dad finally went into town to get out of the way, and I stayed on the couch in the living room. To tell the truth, I wasn't looking forward to dinner myself, even though Uncle Peter is fun and I was beginning to feel hungry for fried chicken.

I felt even more jittery when Miss C. came downstairs for dinner. She always looks pretty, but tonight she was beautiful. She'd piled her hair up on top her head, and she was wearing her best blue dress with Uncle Peter's heart-shaped locket. Mom took one look and went charging back to the kitchen. We could hear her out there mashing —

no, *smashing* — the potatoes and grumbling to herself.

And all that worrying was for nothing! Because practically the first thing Uncle Peter said when he walked in the door was that it looked as if he wasn't going to California after all. The friend who was going to help him find a job had just gotten fired himself!

He looked pretty glum when he told us, so of course everybody started fussing over him and saying how sorry they were — especially Miss Caldwell. It took a while before he cheered up, but the fussing helped, and so did the fried chicken. By the time dinner was over, he was his nice, jokey self again, and Miss C. was so happy she was *glowing*. She kept smiling at Uncle Peter as if she'd forgotten there was anybody else at the table.

So maybe the next few weeks won't be so bad after all. The way Miss C. looks tonight, she isn't going to scold anybody for anything. She's just going to sit up there at her desk and smile, smile, smile.

May 18

On the way home today I was trying to decide whether school was easier when Miss Caldwell was happy or when she was sad. Because when she was sad, school was no fun at all. And now that she's happy, she keeps giving me funny little looks as if she and I have a secret. Every time it happens, Sandra scowls and Marion snickers, and I feel my face is getting red when there's no reason.

May 19

The test questions came today. The minute I saw the big brown envelope on the kitchen table I knew what it was. Mom took it upstairs and put it on Miss C.'s bed where she'd see it right away. The return address on the envelope was Cooper Academy, Haymarket Road, Madison, Wisconsin. I wondered if that will be *my* return address next year. I don't think I can bear it if I don't win the scholarship. I keep telling myself that there are "eighth-grade rural females" all over central Wisconsin who are hoping the same thing. How can I do better than all of them? I'd probably have to get a perfect score on the test, and there's not much chance of that!

May 20

I'm going to write this as fast as I can because I don't want to think about it.

First, as soon as we got to school Miss Caldwell told us — Sandra and Marion and me — that the scholarship test had arrived and we should be at school at nine o'clock the morning of the test. She said we should be sure to get a good night's sleep because the test wasn't going to be easy. Part of it will be true-or-false questions, but most of it will be essay questions. That means a lot of writing. We're supposed to bring two pens and an ink eraser.

I sat with Marion and Sandra at lunchtime, but none of us ate much. Marion was really nervous. She said the test sounded hard, and she didn't know if she'd take it after all. Sandra said that was stupid. She said she could hardly wait until Saturday, and she wasn't worried about the test, as long it was fair and nobody cheated. I knew what she was hinting at, but I didn't care. From the moment Miss C. started talking about the test I felt numb inside, as if I were walking a straight line toward that morning and nothing else mattered.

I said I was going to write this fast, but I keep putting off that bad part. It happened tonight, after supper. Uncle Peter picked up Miss C. about six and I helped with the dishes. Then I went out onto the porch to read until it got dark, which is what I've been doing every evening when it's warm enough. A big brown envelope was sticking out from under the cushion at the end of the swing. I pulled it out, but before I even touched it, I knew what it was. I would have known that envelope anywhere.

Part of me thought Miss C. must have looked over the test before supper, and she forgot to put it away. And part of me thought, Don't be dumb! She left it there because she knew you'd find it. She wants you to see the questions ahead of time. She wants you to be the one who goes to Cooper!

CHAPTER SEVENTEEN

The journal ended there. Jessie, curled up against the head of the bed, thumbed the remaining pages in dismay. There had to be more — but there wasn't.

She shoved the notebook under her pillow and switched off the lamp. Moonlight flooded the room, drawing sharp outlines across the floor but leaving the corners in darkness. For the first time in many nights it didn't occur to Jessie to look for the ghost-woman in the shadows. All her thoughts were on what she'd just read.

What had Eileen done with the test envelope? And why did it matter so much now? Jessie couldn't be sure of the first question, but she knew the answer to the second. It mattered because Grandma Belland was her ideal person, the one she'd always wanted to be like when she grew up. She was smart and pretty and she wasn't afraid of anything. You could depend on her.

Jessie felt disloyal even thinking about the possibility that her grandmother might have cheated.

But she couldn't help remembering what Eileen had written in her first journal: *If only the test weren't so important!* Winning the scholarship had meant everything to Eileen, and studying the questions before she took the test would have made a lot of difference.

Jessie pulled the sheet up to her chin and closed her eyes. Don't think! she told herself. Don't worry about what Eileen did with the test. Don't wonder about what happened to turn Miss Caldwell into the horrible woman in blue. Don't ask any more questions. You might not like the answers.

"Are you going to see Toni today?" Mrs. Belland bustled around the kitchen, full of energy and good cheer. Jessie's father smiled, watching her.

"I think it's going to rain," Jessie said.

"You'll have a long day if you let a few raindrops keep you inside."

"I don't think Toni wants to be friends," Jessie said carefully. "We always get into fights."

"Whatever about?"

Jessie considered telling the truth. One thing we argue about is ghosts, she could say. Toni doesn't believe in them, but I've seen one.

She could imagine her mother's reaction to that.

"Toni has problems," Mr. Belland offered.

118

"The girl has a whopping big chip on her shoulder."

"Well, I can't believe she isn't interested in having a friend practically next door," Mrs. Belland insisted. "After all, she's promised you a kitten, Jessie. I'm sure she wouldn't do that if she didn't like you. And if she's unhappy, maybe you can help her feel better."

Jessie glanced at her father, wishing he'd say more about the chip on Toni's shoulder. It was more than a chip: It was a good-sized log! But he was on his feet and starting toward the living room and the porch, his coffee cup in hand.

"I can drop you off at the farm," Mrs. Belland offered. "I'm leaving right now to make those phone calls."

"It's too early," Jessie said hastily. "Maybe I'll go later."

As soon as her mother left, she went upstairs, took the notebook from under the pillow, and hurried back down to the living room. Hastily, she skimmed the journal one more time, searching for information she might have missed the night before. The blank pages seemed to taunt her with secrets they might have shared.

Out on the porch, the typewriter chattered, stopped, and started again. Jessie put the notebook back in the bottom drawer of the desk and wondered what to do next. Her mother was right; it was going to be a long day.

"I'm going over to Toni's," she called to her father.

"Good girl."

"To see my kitten," Jessie added firmly.

After all, there was a good chance that Toni wouldn't even talk to her. Jessie thought about that as she wheeled her bike down the slope to the road. Toni Draves was like a volcano, ready to explode when you least expected it. And yet she could be nice, too. The hike in the nature preserve had been great at first. Toni had been full of information and eager to share the woods she loved. They'd been friends — until they reached the schoolhouse. What happened after that hadn't been Toni's fault.

When she reached the Draves' mailbox, Jessie slid off her bike and walked up the road. As she rounded the row of spruce trees, a door opened onto the little stoop at the side of the house, and Mr. Draves came out. His tall figure drooped a little, but when he saw Jessie he smiled and waved.

"Morning, neighbor."

Jessie waved back. "Is Toni home?"

"Nope." He ambled toward her, pushing his visored cap to the back of his head. "Left about a half hour ago. Said she felt like a walk, but she took her bike. That means the trail, I guess. She

120

doesn't tell me much, but that trail's always been her favorite place, seems like."

"I'll come back some other time then. I want to find out what the kitten's going to need when I take him home."

"I told her she ought to stop over at your place and ask you to go along with her," Mr. Draves said. "Guess she didn't, huh?"

Jessie shook her head. "It doesn't matter. She probably felt like walking alone."

"That's the trouble!" He kicked a stone in a burst of feeling. "The girl's alone too much. It'd do her good to be with folks once in a while, but she won't try." He looked unhappy. "Easy for me to say — that's what she always tells me. I s'pose she's right, poor kid.

"Maybe you can still catch up to her," he went on, looking at Jessie hopefully. "I hated to see her going off by herself, feeling that way."

"What way?" Jessie asked, though she wasn't sure she wanted to know.

"Toni always thinks she has to prove she's as good as the next one — do you know what I mean? And she sure had a bee in her bonnet this morning. What she expects to prove walking the trail is beyond me, but she was pretty worked up about something. I could tell."

Mr. Draves stopped as they reached the ramp leading up to the barn doors. "You could still catch

121

up with her," he repeated, and now there was no mistaking the pleading note in his voice. "Toni likes you a lot. She might not let on, but she does." He grasped the visor of his cap and pulled it forward, but not before Jessie saw tears in his eyes. "Glad you stopped by, anyway," he mumbled and trudged up the ramp.

Jessie went back to her bike, feeling worse with every step. Mr. Draves might wonder why Toni was excited about a walk in the woods, but Jessie had no doubts. Toni had decided to go back to the schoolhouse and explore it, all by herself. She didn't believe in ghosts, and she was determined to make Jessie feel like a silly scaredy-cat.

Now what? At this very moment, she was sure, Mr. Draves was peeking out one of the barn's little windows, waiting to see whether she would bike down the highway toward the nature preserve or go home. If I don't go, she thought, and the ghost-woman hurts Toni the way she tried to hurt me, it'll be my fault for letting her go there alone!

Quickly, before she could change her mind, she swung down the highway toward the preserve. The sky was getting darker each minute. Streaks of lightning lit up the clouds in the west, and thunder rumbled ominously. Anybody, even a person as stubborn as Toni, ought to admit this was the wrong day for a walk in the woods. Maybe she would appear around the next curve, or the next.

Jessie hoped so, with all her heart. But the road ahead remained empty, and soon the wooden arch marking the entrance to the nature preserve came into view.

There were no cars in the parking lot and only one bicycle in the stand. Jessie propped her bike next to Toni's and walked across the lot to the opening in the trees where the trail began. Her feet felt heavy, as if she were already back in her nightmare, terrified but unable to run away. Her stomach churned.

"Toni? Are you in there?"

Thunder growled again, closer now. As Jessie hesitated at the start of the trail the wind picked up, splattering her with rain and pushing her into the darkness ahead.

CHAPTER EIGHTEEN

Except for the mounting patter of rain in the treetops, the woods were still. The last time Jessie had been here, squirrels had darted across the path and birds sang overhead. Now it seemed as if every living thing had gone into hiding to wait out the storm.

She tried to remember how long it had taken to walk to the schoolhouse. Not more than a half hour, she decided. The panicky trip back — it had been raining then, too — had been much faster.

She started down the trail. Above the path the branches trembled and danced in the wind. At every curve Jessie hesitated, then forced herself to go on. Once, when she looked back, it seemed for a sickening moment that the trail had actually closed behind her, as it had in her nightmares.

Then the clearing appeared in front of her. Tall grass bent under the rain, and the little schoolhouse seemed to be riding the waves of a green sea. Jessie shrank back as lightning blazed. The schoolhouse shimmered in the burst of light, its outline wavering, its door swinging in the wind.

"Toni!" Thunder drowned out Jessie's cry. She shouted again, but this time the wind swallowed up the sound. If Toni was inside the schoolhouse — and where else could she be? — she wouldn't be able to hear.

Jessie waded through the grass, her eyes fixed on the open door. The wind urged her along, and as she reached the steps lightning cracked the sky above the bell tower.

"Toni! It's me, Jessie!"

Clinging to the porch rail, Jessie wondered if Toni might be playing a trick on her. Perhaps she'd been looking out a window and was waiting now, just inside the door, ready to leap out when Jessie entered. It was possible.

A burst of anger sent Jessie clattering up the steps. She wasn't a coward! She wasn't! Anyone would be afraid who had actually seen the woman in blue and felt the force of her hatred. Toni was the stupid one, charging into danger she didn't understand.

A quick glance told her Toni was not waiting to pounce. The schoolroom was dark but alive with sound. Rain streamed down the dusty windows and rattled on the roof. Jessie looked for something to prop the door open with and found a brick, probably left for that purpose, in a corner.

"Toni?" She edged along the front row of desks

to the center of the room. A leaf skittered ahead of her, blown through the open door.

"Come on, Toni, where are you?" Jessie hardly recognized her own squeaky-thin, quivery voice.

At the back of the room the door that led to the bathrooms and closet was a forbidding black rectangle. Jessie walked toward it slowly, her heart thudding. She felt as if she were dreaming again, but this time there was no waking up. The doorway drew her like a magnet, forcing her to find out what lay beyond it.

"Toni, if you're hiding in there, I'll never talk to you again. This isn't funny. You're being mean — "

Jessie peered into the dark hall one way, then the other. Too late, she saw the gaping hole in the floor right ahead of her. The toes of her left foot came down in empty space, and she teetered wildly. With a squeal of terror she threw herself backward, hitting the door frame as she fell.

For a moment she crouched on the floor, too terrified even to cry. Gradually she was able to make out a trapdoor leaning against the opposite wall. The opening in front of it was several feet long and about four feet wide.

Like a grave! Jessie shuddered.

"Toni?" Trembling, she crawled to the edge of the hole and peered down. At first, she couldn't see the bottom, but after a few seconds her eyes became used to the darkness. A roaring began in her head, louder than the thunder that shook the schoolhouse, and she clutched the edge of the opening to steady herself. Toni lay at the bottom of the hole. Her eyes were closed, her face gray-white except for the blood that streaked her forehead and one cheek.

CHAPTER
NINETEEN

Jessie rocked back on her heels. She'd never seen a dead person, but Toni's grayish face and the awkward twist of her body made her look like a lifeless doll. If she wasn't dead, she must be badly hurt.

Trembling, Jessie peered over the edge again. The opening in the floor was a kind of huge box or pit that was lined with metal. The box was at least six feet deep, with a single shelf stretching along either side near the bottom. Toni had come back to this hallway the first time they visited the schoolhouse, but she hadn't noticed the trapdoor in the floor. Since then, someone had opened it and left it that way.

"Toni? Toni, can you hear me? I'm going to get your dad, okay?"

Jessie cringed as thunder crashed close by. When she looked down again, Toni's hand was in a different position, close to her chin. But her eyes were still closed and she gave no sign of having heard.

Jessie stood up and looked out into the class-room. More than anything, she wanted to run away from this place. It was the right thing to do; she couldn't rescue Toni all by herself. But *what if she wakes up while I'm gone? She'll be all alone and scared and she won't know help will be coming soon. I've got to make her understand. I've got to make her hear.*

She knelt next to the pit and dangled her legs over the side. The distance to the shelf was greater than it had appeared from above and, as she low-ered herself, the metal edges of the box cut into her fingers. She clung to the rim and stretched one leg, then the other. At last her right toe brushed the shelf. She slid down until only her head and shoulders were above the level of the floor.

Panic swept over her when she realized how far she'd dropped. It was going to be *hard* to get out again, maybe impossible. She'd have to hitch herself up and swing sideways, hook a foot over the edge, pull herself up. . . .

Something moved in the hallway at the far end of the pit. Jessie turned and almost slipped from her perch on the shelf. With the slow step of a sleepwalker, the woman in blue was moving to-ward her out of the shadows. She looked very tall in the narrow hall, a terrifying ghost-giant. The pretty face was expressionless, but when she bent and reached for the edge of the trapdoor, the corners of her mouth lifted in a cruel smile.

"NO!"

Jessie screamed and tumbled backward as the trapdoor swung shut. One outstretched arm struck the opposite side of the box, breaking her fall slightly, and then she was lying at the bottom of the pit. Darkness settled over her like a musty blanket.

"Get off," grumbled a voice in the dark. "That hurts."

Jessie struggled to sit up. She had landed on Toni's legs. Shifting clumsily, she moved backward until she was resting on the metal floor at one end of the pit, her knees scrunched up to her chin.

"Toni, are you awake?" She whispered the words, picturing a ghostly eavesdropper overhead. "It's me, Jessie."

"Feel awful," Toni groaned. "Want to go home. Right now."

Jessie took a deep breath. There was a familiar, testy note in Toni's voice that was reassuring.

"We can't go home yet. We're in some kind of storage place under the school floor. You fell in and then — " Jessie hesitated, "and then I fell in, too."

"Dumb." Toni groaned. "I'm tired. Want to go home now."

Jessie tried to stay calm. Her head ached and her elbow was sore where she'd struck the side of the box, but the bumps and bruises weren't important. The only thing that mattered now was getting out of the box, and she was going to have to do it alone. Toni was alive but obviously not thinking clearly.

When would someone come looking for them? Jessie's heart sank as she realized her father would assume she was safe and dry at the Draves' farm. If the storm continued, Toni's father might get worried when they didn't return, but how long would it take before he decided to search for them? And then he'd have to drive to the nature preserve, walk the path to the schoolhouse . . .

"Hot in here," Toni muttered irritably. "Open the window."

It *was* hot, but Jessie shivered in her corner of the box. Her wet clothes felt clammy, and a mixture of raindrops and sweat rolled down her cheeks. This was like her nightmares, she thought, only much worse. In her last nightmare the schoolhouse door had swung shut, and she had felt as if she were going to suffocate. . . .

"Oh, no!" The words slipped out before she could stop them.

131

Toni shifted uneasily. "What? What's wrong?"

Jessie couldn't answer. For the first time, the full horror of what had happened struck her. She and Toni were in a box with metal walls and a heavy wooden lid. No air could get in. If they had to wait a long time for someone to find them, they might suffocate.

She put out her hand, found the shelf, and pulled herself up on it, pressing against the wall to keep her balance. She didn't care if the ghost-woman was waiting and watching in the hallway. Nothing mattered except lifting the trapdoor — even a crack — enough to let in fresh air.

When her head touched the wooden panels she crouched, pressed her hands against the door, and pushed as hard as she could. The door didn't move. Again and again she strained, till her shoulders ached and the sore elbow throbbed. It was no use. Either the trapdoor was too heavy or someone — something — was holding it down.

"Jessie? Is that you, Jessie?" Toni sounded drowsy now. "What's wrong? What're you doing?"

Jessie rubbed her shoulders. "I was trying to get some air," she said shakily. "Don't worry. I'll try again in a minute."

"Take a nap," Toni advised. She yawned. "That's what I'm going to do."

Jessie stood up on the bench, head bent, and pushed again. She paused, trying to picture how the trapdoor had looked when it was open. Thick wooden panels, hinges . . . that was it! She must be pushing against the hinged side of the door. Of course it wouldn't open.

Quickly she worked her way to the end of the shelf, stepped down into the open space beyond Toni's feet, and climbed onto the shelf on the other side. When she stood up again, her chest ached, and she felt dizzy. She wondered if she was going to faint.

Keep trying, Jessie. Don't you dare give up!

Jessie blinked back tears. She had heard the words as clearly as if Grandma Belland were there beside her. Gritting her teeth, she reached up again and pushed with all her might. The door moved slightly. Another push, and this time she raised it nearly an inch before it thudded down.

Was it the weight of the door itself that had slammed it shut, or had someone pushed it? She couldn't be sure, but Jessie was triumphant. For a couple of seconds she had felt the wind blowing through the schoolhouse and had heard the pounding rain. As long as she could lift the door even a little, she and Toni wouldn't suffocate.

Breathless, she sank down on the shelf and rubbed her arms. The roar of the storm had made

133

her realize how soundproof the box was when the trapdoor was closed. If Mr. Draves came looking for them, they wouldn't hear him calling. If they shouted for help, he wouldn't hear.

Jessie, don't you dare give up!

What she needed was a prop to hold the door open a crack. It would have to be something hard — a stick — or a shoe! She slipped off one sneaker and worked the laces out of the holes. Then she took off the other sneaker and stuffed it into the first one, using the shoelaces to bind them together. A couple of worn old sneakers weren't much of a prop, but it was the best she could do. She wouldn't give up.

She stood up on the shelf, tucked the sneakers between her chin and her chest, and pushed with all her strength. One inch! Two! For a second, she held the full weight of the door on her right hand and used her left to thrust the shoes into the narrow opening. This time when she dropped her arms a strip of grayish light remained.

"JESSIE, ARE YOU IN HERE?"

Jessie gasped. She wondered if she was imagining her father's voice, as she had imagined Grandma Belland's.

"JESSIE!"

She wasn't imagining it. Jessie screamed, over and over again, until her voice cracked and Toni whimpered unhappily. Then her screams were choked off in a storm of tears. The trapdoor flew open, and a beam of yellow light swept down into the box. Jessie stared up into her father's horrified face. Mr. Draves was crouched close beside him.

Before she knew what was happening, she had been lifted up into the hallway, and the two men were down in the box. There was a hint of smoke in the rush of air from the open door at the front of the schoolroom.

"Get out of the way up there."

Jessie scuttled backward as her father and Mr. Draves lifted Toni out of the box and then climbed out themselves.

"Now, move!" her father ordered. "Get out of here, Jess. We'll be right behind you. The bell tower was hit by lightning a couple of minutes ago — the whole place may go up!"

Jessie darted between desks to the front of the room. When she reached the door she stopped and held it for the men who were carrying Toni.

"Good girl," her father panted. "Okay, now run!"

Later, Jessie would wonder what it was that had made her hesitate for even a moment and look back. Smoke whirled and twisted through the schoolroom. Near the back of the room, the woman in blue sat at a desk, her blonde head resting on her folded arms. Her face was very white, and her eyes were closed.

"Jessie! I said, move!"

The figure vanished. Jessie dashed down the schoolhouse steps. Rain pelted her cheeks and the wind pushed against her with bullying power. She felt as if she could run forever.

CHAPTER TWENTY

"Oh, my, I know all about that old storage bin!" Grandma Belland exclaimed. "Every June we packed our textbooks and other supplies down there for the summer. I can't think of anything worse than being trapped in it!"

Jessie lay on the couch in the living room. Wrapped in a bathrobe and sipping hot soup, she still couldn't stop shivering. Her mother and grandmother sat close by, watching her as if she might disappear if they looked away.

"Well, I don't understand what you girls were doing in the school, anyway," Mrs. Belland said. "Of all days to go for a walk in the woods! And how could you *both* fall into that dreadful hole? You're lucky you weren't killed. When your father called and said you were somewhere out in this storm — he didn't know where — I dropped what I was doing and dashed out of the store without a word to anyone. I don't know what Mr. Andersen thought."

Grandma Belland reached over to pat her hand. "I felt the same way when I got Jessie's letter this morning. All I could think of was that something awful was going to happen, and I had to come home immediately. And I was right, wasn't I? I just hope Toni isn't badly hurt, poor child."

Jessie's mother stood up, looking more disturbed than ever. "That letter!" she scolded. "Your grandmother let your father and me read it, Jessie. Ghosts, for goodness' sake! How could you have bothered her with all that nonsense? If you were frightened you should have told us." She bent to touch Jessie's forehead with her fingertips and then hurried toward the kitchen. "I'm going to get dinner started. Your father and Mr. Draves will be starving by the time they get back from the hospital. Maybe they'll have Toni with them," she added over her shoulder. "I hope so!"

"I hope so, too," Grandma Belland said softly. "But right now — " she hitched her chair closer to the couch — "do you feel able to talk a little, Jessie? Or maybe just listen? Because your letter gave me a great deal to think about. You see, I've never believed in ghosts either."

"Do you now?" Jessie asked anxiously.

"I think I used to know your lady in blue."

Jessie sat up. She felt as if a huge weight had slipped from her shoulders. "She was there in the school today, Grandma. She closed the trapdoor when I was trying to help Toni. And I saw her again after Dad and Mr. Draves got us out. It was so weird — she was sitting at a desk with her head down, as if she'd fallen asleep."

"Was she, indeed?" Grandma nodded thoughtfully. "Describe her for me again, dear."

"She has a pretty face and long blonde hair. And she's so angry-looking — as if she just *hates* me. Why should Miss Caldwell hate me, Grandma? She never even knew me."

Grandma Belland's brown eyes widened. "Miss Caldwell? Oh, my dear! Miss Caldwell isn't your ghost. As a matter of fact, she's very much alive. She's living in a nursing home in Madison now and she's still bright as a button. I've visited her there several times. . . . Jessie, there's something I want to show you."

Jessie leaned back on the cushions and closed her eyes, while Grandma Belland hurried down the hall to the den. Rain pattered against the windows, and from the kitchen came sizzling sounds and her mother's quick steps. Jessie's head felt heavy, resisting all attempts to make sense of what she had just heard. It was enough to know Grandma believed her.

When Grandma returned, she was carrying a bulky photo album. She laid it on Jessie's lap.

"I want you to look at these pictures, Jess. That first one is of me, on the day I graduated from eighth grade. It could just as well be you, couldn't it?"

Jessie nodded. Except for the way they dressed, thirteen-year-old Eileen and twelve-year-old Jessie might be identical twins.

"Now this one," Grandma pointed. "Miss Caldwell and I, that same day."

Jessie stared at the second snapshot. Miss Caldwell was blonde and very pretty, just as Eileen had described in the journals. But she was short — no more than an inch taller than her pupil — and her round, dimpled face was nothing like that of the woman in the blue dress.

"You don't have to say anything," Grandma murmured. She turned a page of the album. "Look at this picture, Jess. It was taken on graduation day, too, just before the ceremony was to begin."

The three girls in their white dresses and the two boys in white shirts and dark trousers were grouped on the schoolhouse steps. Miss Caldwell stood on the porch behind them. They were squinting into the sun, and all but one were smiling.

Jessie gasped. She pointed a shaky finger at the tall light-haired girl on the left who stared soberly at the photographer.

"That's her, Grandma! That's the ghost — she's that girl, all grown up!"

"I thought so," Grandma said. "And that's Sandra. At least, that was the name she picked out for herself because she thought it sounded glamorous. When we were in fourth grade we all experimented with different names. I was Gloria for a couple of months, and Marion was Marilyn. Sandra kept her new name and insisted we use it. Her real name was Sophie Gorder. She lived right next door to us, just as her granddaughter does now."

"Toni? You mean Sandra was Toni's grandmother?" Jessie stared unbelievingly at the face that had haunted her dreams. "But why would Sandra try to hurt me — and why would she make Toni fall into the storage bin? Her own granddaughter!"

Grandma closed the album and laid it on the floor. "I don't think the storage bin was left open to trap Toni, dear. I'm afraid it was meant for you."

"But why?" Jessie wailed. "It doesn't make sense."

Grandma put her arm around Jessie's shoulders. "Of course it doesn't. Hatred doesn't make sense. But when I read your letter — well, as I told you, I've never believed in ghosts, but I knew something very strange was happening. Your lady in blue sounded so much like Sandra. And since you look the way I did in eighth grade, I began to wonder if your coming to this house to live could have brought an old hatred to life again. Because Sandra did hate me, dear. When Miss Caldwell announced that I'd won the scholarship to the Cooper Academy, Sandra made an ugly scene. In front of the whole school she accused me of cheating and Miss Caldwell of helping me. And that wasn't the end of it. Several times over the years I was at Cooper she sent me cruel little notes telling me I had ruined her life. I remember feeling *sick* every time I saw her handwriting on an envelope."

"But she went to high school, too, didn't she?"

Grandma nodded. "She went to Willow High, but she dropped out after a year or two. I heard she'd married a man who worked on her family's farm. By the time I graduated from Cooper, she'd had a baby — Toni's mother. I hoped she'd gotten over her anger, but we never spoke again. I went to the university — that was where I met your grandpa — and afterward we bought a house in Willow and I taught in the high school. I saw Sandra in town occasionally, but she always turned away quickly, as if she couldn't bear to look at me.

"And then one day I heard something terrible. It happened on a Saturday, while her husband was away buying livestock. She put her little girl into her playpen and left. Her husband and the sheriff searched everywhere, but it wasn't until Monday morning that she was found — in the schoolhouse. She was dead — sitting at her old desk with an empty pill bottle beside her."

"She killed herself?" Jessie shuddered. "Oh, Grandma."

"It was a dreadful thing," Grandma said. "For a long time I felt guilty, realizing how bitter she'd been and wondering if I could have done something to help her. When I read your letter, and you mentioned the heart-shaped pendant, it brought back that whole painful time. I was terrified for you!"

"But the pendant was Miss Caldwell's," Jessie interrupted. "You wrote about it in the journal."

"That's right," Grandma agreed. "And she treasured it, even though I think she was beginning to accept the fact that Uncle Peter was never going to marry and settle down. The day after we graduated, the eighth-graders — all five of us — went back to school to help pack up the books for the summer. It was a dusty job, and Miss Caldwell took off the pendant and her ring and put on a smock before we began. When we were ready to go home, the pendant was gone. We looked everywhere. Miss Caldwell was very upset. I think we all guessed what had happened to it — Sandra had been sulky all day and had come to help only because her parents insisted. We couldn't prove she'd taken it, but we knew. Later, Marion told me Sandra was wearing the pendant when she died."

"But *why* did she kill herself?" Jessie wondered. "Just because she didn't get the scholarship . . . ?"

"The scholarship was only the beginning, I'm afraid," Grandma said sadly. "She was deeply disappointed, and it was easier to blame someone else than to go on trying, I guess. That kind of thinking can become a habit, Jessie. As the years passed, she became so bitter that life just wasn't worth living."

Suddenly Jessie was so exhausted that she could hardly keep her eyes open. There was more she wanted to ask her grandmother — one particularly important question — but she couldn't make herself say the words. Not tonight.

Grandma stood up, smiling. "Go ahead and sleep, dear. You're not afraid of having a nightmare now, are you?"

Jessie remembered the way the ghost had looked, sitting at her desk in the smoke-filled schoolhouse. For the first time her face had worn a peaceful expression.

"I think she's gone, Grandma." Jessie couldn't

say why she was so sure. "Maybe she finally figured out that I'm not you — and you're not that girl she hates anymore."

"Maybe so," Grandma said softly. "I'd like to believe she's at peace after all this. . . ."

Jessie didn't hear the end of the sentence. She was fast asleep.

CHAPTER
TWENTY-ONE

"My, my, you're smiling in your sleep," said a familiar voice. "Your dreams must be improving, Jess."

"They are." Jessie stretched and sat up. She looked around wonderingly. "What happened last night, Grandma? I don't remember eating, or coming up to bed, or anything."

"That's because you slept right through dinner, my dear. And would you believe your father carried you upstairs?" Grandma Belland shook her head in amazement. "He puffed and panted a lot, but he did it. When that boy makes up his mind to do a thing, it gets done." She put her hand to her ear, and Jessie heard the typewriter tapping furiously downstairs.

"Is Toni okay?"

"She will be, but the doctor wants her to stay in the hospital for a couple of days. I thought you and I would drive over to Marshton to see her today, before I go back to Madison. I think we

146

should tell her what we talked about last night."

Jessie rolled her eyes. "Toni doesn't believe in ghosts, Grandma. No way!"

"Well, she's going to listen, just the same," Grandma said firmly. "From what your father told me last night, Toni is a very unhappy girl. She has to decide right now whether she's going to go on blaming her difficulties on other people or make up her mind to keep trying. Hearing her grandma's story may help, don't you think?"

"Are you going to tell her everything?" Jessie slid down under the sheet again and lay facing the portrait of Eileen. It was easier than looking into the lively brown eyes regarding her from the foot of the bed.

"What did you think I might leave out?" Grandma wondered.

Jessie took a deep breath. "About Miss Caldwell leaving the test where you'd find it. I found that journal in your desk. Are you going to tell Toni about that?"

Grandma didn't reply for a moment. Then she came around the bed and stood close to Jessie. "Yes, I'll tell her that — *especially* that," she said quietly. "Finding that test, knowing I could see the questions in advance — that was the biggest temptation of my young life, Jessie. I guess you know

I wanted that scholarship more than anything. And I came very close to taking the test out of the envelope and reading it. It would have been so easy. But I didn't do it, and I've never stopped being glad I didn't. If Sandra had been right when she accused me of cheating, it would have taken all the joy out of going to Cooper. In fact, it would have changed my whole life. I didn't write in my journal after that night, but I've always kept the notebook in my desk where I would see it and be reminded of how close I came to making a terrible mistake."

Jessie closed her eyes and yawned. She didn't want Grandma to guess how relieved she was. "I knew it," she mumbled. "I just knew it."

"Did you?"

Jessie peeked and saw that Grandma was smiling.

"You take another little catnap, dear. I'll give you — let's see — one more hour. Will that be enough? Then off we go to Marshton."

"One more hour," Jessie sighed contentedly. This time the yawn was a real one.

They stood at the edge of the sunlit clearing and looked at the schoolhouse. Some of the shingles close to the bell tower were scorched, and there were boards nailed across the closed door.

"Time to tear the old place down, I think," Grandma said softly, *"before someone else gets hurt. It makes me sad to see it like this."*

Jessie was surprised to discover she felt nothing at all. It was just an old schoolhouse. Nothing to be afraid of.